look for me by moonlight

look for me by moonlight

MARY DOWNING HAHN

HOUGHTON MIFFLIN HARCOURT
BOSTON · NEW YORK

For information about permission to reproduce selections from
this book, write to Permissions, Houghton Mifflin Company,
215 Park Avenue South, New York, New York 10003.

Graphia and the Graphia logo are registered trademarks of
Houghton Mifflin Harcourt Publishing Company.

Library of Congress Cataloging-in-Publication Data
Hahn, Mary Downing.
  Look for me by moonlight / by Mary Downing Hahn.
    p. cm.
  Summary: While staying at the remote and reputedly haunted Maine
inn run by her father and pregnant stepmother, sixteen-year-old Cynda
feels increasingly isolated from her father' s new family and finds solace
in the attentions of a charming but mysterious guest.
    HC ISBN-13: 978-0-395-69843-3 PA ISBN-13: 978-0-547-07616-4
    [1. Horror stories. 2. Vampires—Fiction. 3. Ghosts—Fiction.
4. Stepfamilies—Fiction. 5. Hotels, motels, etc.—Fiction. 6. Maine—
Fiction.] I. Title.
PZ7.H1256Lo 1995
[Fic] — dc20
94-21892
    CIP   AC

Printed in the USA
EB 10 9 8 7 6 5 4 3 2 1

For
NANCY AND BEV
With thanks for all the encouragement

Then look for me by moonlight,
Watch for me by moonlight,
I'll come to thee by moonlight, though hell
should bar the way.

"The Highwayman," Alfred Noyes

1

Sometimes you can pinpoint the exact moment in your life when things begin to go wrong. For me, it was the day my father left my mother. I was six years old, too young to understand what was happening except that it involved a student in one of Dad's literature classes. A girl named Susan. Because of her, he was moving out of our house. I cried and begged him to stay, I swore I'd be good, but nothing I said or did made any difference. Dad packed his bags and his books and kissed me goodbye.

"I love you, Cynda," he said. "No matter where I live, I'll always be your father, and you'll always be my daughter. Nothing will change."

Of course, it wasn't true. A year later, Dad moved to Maine with Susan and I stayed in Maryland with Mom. That meant he was suddenly almost a thousand miles away. It also meant I saw less and less of him.

Not long after Dad married Susan, Mom married Steve, and things changed again. We became a Navy family, hopscotching all over America. California, Florida, Virginia—we never stayed in one place long enough for me to make friends, settle down, and feel comfortable.

When Steve announced we were going to Italy for three years, I flat-out rebelled. Giving up all pretense of being a mature sixteen-year-old, I threw a major temper tantrum which resulted in a series of phone calls between my mother and my father. The end result was an invitation to stay with Dad for at least six months, maybe longer if things worked out.

Mom's role in setting up the visit surprised me. She'd never forgiven Dad for falling in love with Susan. Nor did she approve of his career. In addition to writing best-selling mysteries, he ran an old inn on the Maine coast—occupations my mother denounced as fiscally irresponsible, proof of Dad's immaturity and selfishness.

Later, when I had time to think about it, I came to the conclusion that Mom and Steve had decided Italy would be more fun without me. To be candid, things hadn't been good in our house since I turned thirteen and, as Mom put it, lost my mind overnight. Which meant I changed from an obedient child who never gave anyone a second's trouble into an obnoxious teenager who left wet towels on the bathroom floor and dirty dishes in front of the television, played loud music, and argued about everything from politics to curfews. Maybe Mom thought it was Dad's turn to cope with me. Maybe I was her revenge.

Whatever her reasons, Mom put me on a plane to Maine one cold January day. As I left National Airport in Washington behind, I tried to convince myself I was going to a new and better life with Dad, but deep down inside I wasn't so sure. I hadn't seen my father for almost two years, hadn't talked to him about anything important for longer than that. Worse yet, I'd never met his wife or their son, now five years old. I might not like Susan, she might not like me. Todd might be spoiled and bratty.

By the time my plane landed, I'd had more time to think (and worry) than I'd expected. Thanks to winter storms buffeting the coast from Virginia to Nova Scotia, my flight had been delayed, diverted, and unexpectedly stranded in Boston for two hours. I'd eaten lousy food and washed it down with even worse coffee. I'd read a three-hundred-page novel whose plot I'd already forgotten. I'd been pushed and jostled and propositioned by strangers. Not to mention bounced from one air pocket to another all the way to Bangor.

Jumpy, jangled, and tense, I was too strung out with anxiety to join the passengers mobbing the aisle. I stayed in my seat, closed my eyes, and tried to relax. In a few minutes, I'd come face to face with a father who might not even recognize me. I was going to stay with him for six months. Twenty-four weeks, more or less. A hundred and seventy-eight days. What would we do? What would we say? A lot could go wrong in half a year.

The doubts I'd swept under the rug began to crawl out, bigger and uglier than ever. How did Dad feel about me? Did he really want me? Or was he just doing Mom a favor? He had Susan now. And Todd.

He didn't need me. Neither did Mom. She had Steve. But who did I have? Not even a boyfriend.

"Are you all right, sweetie?"

I looked up to see a flight attendant staring down at me. Red-faced with embarrassment, I hastily gathered my belongings. While I'd been brooding, everyone else had gotten off the plane. I was the only passenger still on board.

"It was a terrible flight," the attendant said as if bad weather explained everything. Chattering cheerfully about air turbulence, she followed me to the plane's exit, wished me well, and waved goodbye.

I expected to see Dad at the gate, but he wasn't there. No one was. The waiting area was deserted, the check-in desk unstaffed. Discarded newspapers and rows of empty seats gave the place a surreal look. It could have been a set for a movie about the end of the world.

Fighting panic, I reminded myself that Dad lived way up the coast, close to Canada. The snow had probably delayed him. He'd be here soon. I sat down and leafed aimlessly through my book. After a few minutes, my imagination began churning out increasingly scary scenarios. The storm had closed the roads. Dad had given up and gone back home. He couldn't call because the telephone lines were down. Maybe he'd had an accident. Maybe he was in the hospital. Maybe he'd forgotten I was coming.

What was I going to do? It was dark and cold outside. I knew no one in Bangor. I didn't have enough money to buy a return ticket. And even if I did go

4

back to Washington, where would I stay? Our house was rented. Like a little kid, I wanted my mother, but she was on her way to Italy, blithely assuming I was safe with Dad.

An hour passed. I cried for a while, then I got mad. People arrived to meet a flight from Albany. I hated them for not being my father. I hated my father for not being them.

Just as the Albany passengers deplaned, Dad came hurrying toward me. He looked the same as I remembered, ruddy-faced and with a full beard. "Cynda, I'm so sorry," he said, giving me a hug. "The roads were terrible—accidents all the way to Bangor, cars and trucks everywhere. I'm lucky I got through."

I clung to him, crying again in spite of myself. "I was scared something had happened to you," I sobbed. "I thought you'd gone off the road, I was afraid you'd forgotten . . ."

Dad apologized again, adding, "Don't be silly, honey. Nothing could have stopped me from getting here. Neither rain nor sleet nor whatever, as the post office puts it."

I tried to smile, to make our reunion go the way I'd planned, but all the clever things I'd meant to say dissolved into a silly jumble of platitudes and corny clichés.

"You look great," Dad said, probably to cover up the awkward silence developing between us. "Prettier than ever, just plain lovely."

I shrugged Dad's compliments away, too embarrassed to thank him, and followed him to Baggage

Claim. On the way, I glanced at my reflection in a plate-glass window, hoping to see what he saw. There I was—a tall, thin girl with a pale, narrow face and long, dark hair, tangled from sleeping on the plane. Gawky. All arms and legs and feet. A loping walk Mom had tried unsuccessfully to correct with ballet lessons.

Who was Dad kidding? At sixteen, I was far from pretty, even further from lovely. Just plain was more like it.

After we found my suitcases, we loaded them into an old Volvo station wagon and headed north toward Underhill Inn, dodging in and out of snowstorms all the way to the coast. I was too tired to say much, so I let Dad do most of the talking, something he obviously enjoyed. He began by telling me how much Susan and Todd were looking forward to meeting me. I hoped it was true. Next he gave a long account of Susan's many talents, which included decorating, bookkeeping, and sewing.

"You'll love her," he said confidently. "And wait till you see Todd. You'll adore him, Cynda. Everybody does."

Still talking, Dad accelerated to pass a log truck, and I closed my eyes, certain the chains holding the logs would break and we'd be crushed to death under the load. The Volvo fishtailed on the snowy road, but Dad was too absorbed in telling me about Todd to notice I was frightened. If my father was to be believed, my half brother was a child prodigy, sensitive and imaginative as well as charming.

How nice, I thought, but what about me? Was I

special too? Or was I merely the daughter he left behind when he fell in love with Susan?

After we turned off Route 9, Dad asked if I'd like to stop for coffee. "We still have about thirty miles to go, and I could use a break."

"Coffee and something to eat," I said, grabbing the chance to keep Dad to myself a little longer. Maybe we'd relax over coffee and feel comfortable with each other. Maybe he'd ask a question that would open my heart. Maybe he'd at least stop talking about Todd.

"There's the Seaside Diner's sign." Dad pointed at a pink glow in the sky I'd mistaken for the northern lights. "It's the only place open at this hour."

A few minutes later, Dad maneuvered the Volvo into a parking place behind a pickup truck so coated with road salt I couldn't read the license plate. "Welcome to the thriving metropolis of Ferrington," he said.

Mountains of plowed snow hid most of the town, but I made out a row of dark buildings, among them a beauty salon, a small grocery, a pharmacy, and a video rental store. The rest of the shops were boarded up, closed for the season. Or maybe forever.

The diner was across the street. Even though it was early January, red cardboard letters still hung in the steamy windows, spelling out a crooked Merry Christmas. The huge neon sign splashed the snow with colored light.

Inside, three old men sat at the counter, drinking coffee and smoking. Otherwise the place was deserted. Even the jukebox was silent.

"What can I bring you, Mr. Bennett?" The middle-aged waitress spoke to Dad but stared at me with undisguised curiosity. "The chowder's excellent tonight. Thick and creamy, lots of clams—just the way you like it."

"Sounds great." Dad looked at me. "How about you, Cynda?"

I said I'd have the chowder too, and Dad turned to the waitress. "Two bowls, please, and a pot of your finest coffee, Gina, as hot and strong as you can make it."

While she jotted down our order, Gina kept her eyes on me. Finally Dad noticed. "This is my daughter, Cynthia," he said. "Cynda for short. She just flew in from Washington, D.C."

Gina smiled as if Dad had merely confirmed something she already knew. "Martha said you were coming today."

"Martha Bigelow," Dad explained to me. "She helps Susan with the cleaning. We couldn't run the inn without her."

By the time Gina returned with our order, Dad was drawing a diagram of Underhill Inn on a paper napkin, pointing out various rooms and talking about the building's history.

"This part dates all the way back to 1781, but the rest of it just grew over the years." Dad's finger moved from square to square. "A room here, a room there."

Gina set the bowls down, taking care not to spill any chowder on Dad's floor plan. "You should have

8

seen Underhill before your father bought it, Cynda. The place had been empty for years. Windows and doors boarded up, roof fallen in, swallows roosting in the chimneys . . . a real ruin."

"Now, Gina, it wasn't as bad as that," Dad said. "The walls were sound, and so was the foundation. All Underhill needed was a little love—and several thousand dollars' worth of work."

"It's a marvel what you and Mrs. Bennett have done," Gina insisted. Turning to me, she said, "In the summer, the inn's packed with folks from all over the map—California, Hawaii, Florida. Some Germans stayed for a whole month last August. Lovely people."

She paused to wipe a spot on the table. "It's a lonely place in the winter, though. Very bleak, nobody around, nothing to do."

"That's when I love Underhill the most," Dad said quickly. "No guests, no interruptions, plenty of time to write."

"I guess it's all in how you look at it," Gina said, "but you couldn't pay me to stay there. Not in the winter. Maybe not even in the summer."

"Why not?" I stared at her, startled by her bluntness.

Gina glanced at Dad. "Haven't you told Cynda about the ghost?"

"You know what I think of that nonsense." Dad winked at me but I didn't return his smile.

"Is Underhill haunted?" I asked Gina.

"Most folks around here think so." She frowned

at Dad. "If you don't believe me, ask Martha Bigelow. She often feels something watching her when she's upstairs cleaning. Gives her goose bumps all over."

A little shiver raced up and down my spine, but Dad snorted with disbelief. Gina leaned across the table and gazed into his eyes. "Don't tell me you've never noticed anything strange, Mr. Bennett."

He shook his head emphatically, but Gina wasn't satisfied. "How about your guests, then?"

"They complain about the weather, they fuss about the mattresses and the TV reception, but nobody has ever said a word about ghosts." Dad slid his empty cup toward Gina. "How about a refill?"

Gina took the hint and left to get the coffee pot, but I wasn't ready to drop the subject. "How can you be so sure it's all nonsense, Dad? Maybe Mrs. Bigelow is psychic, maybe there really is a ghost. . . ."

"I have more important things to worry about. Paying the mortgage, for instance. Keeping my guests happy. Hoping the furnace will make it through another winter."

"But you write mysteries," I persisted, surprised by his attitude. "Wouldn't a haunted inn be a good setting for a story?"

Dad looked insulted. "My novels are serious police procedurals," he said stiffly. "They deal with murder, arson, armed robbery, and drugs. The supernatural is Stephen King's territory. Not mine."

Rebuked, I lowered my head and began to eat my chowder. I'd say no more about ghosts to Dad. I wanted him to think well of me, to brag about me the way he bragged about Todd. I didn't dare risk lowering his opinion of me by admitting Gina had scared me.

When Gina returned, I thought she might say more about Underhill, but Dad's attitude must have discouraged her, too. She made a comment about the record-breaking cold, totaled our bill, and walked off with Dad's tip jingling in her pocket.

As we left Ferrington behind, I found myself wishing Dad lived in one of the big old houses we'd passed on our way out of town. They'd looked as warm and welcoming as illustrations in a child's picture book. Surely no ghosts lurked in their cozy rooms.

Dad caught me shivering and smiled, mistaking the reason. "Maine takes some getting used to, Cynda. We only have two seasons, you know. Eleven months of winter and one of summer."

I forced myself to laugh, but my father's joke didn't dispel the odd, lingering dread I felt. Staring into the darkness ahead, I wondered why people thought Underhill was haunted. Since I couldn't ask Dad, I'd talk to Mrs. Bigelow the next time she came to clean the inn. Maybe she'd tell me what sort of ghost watched her from the shadows.

2

The farther we drove, the darker and lonelier the night seemed. No stores, no houses, just an occasional mailbox marking a driveway. Snowy fields crosshatched with woods. A stone wall. An old barn. Nothing to light our way but the moon, sailing in and out of clouds, as pale and regal as a queen crowned with stars.

Gazing at the sky, Dad said, "'The moving moon went up the sky, And nowhere did abide.'"

"'Softly she was going up,'" I added. "'And a star or two beside—'"

Dad looked pleased. "You know Coleridge."

For one lovely moment, I felt as close to Dad as I'd hoped to. He'd quoted a line of poetry that floated through my head whenever I looked at the moon wandering across the heavens, unfixed, homeless, alone.

Several minutes later, Dad came to a stop on a high rise of land overlooking fields of snow. The ocean glimmered on the horizon, spangled with moonlight. "There it is," he said. "Underhill Inn."

Below us, a three-story stone building stood by itself at the end of a long driveway. Smoke rose from double chimneys. In each window a candle glowed, the only lights in the surrounding darkness.

"An innkeeper's tradition," Dad explained. "Candles to guide the weary traveler—not that many come this way in the winter."

On a summer day with flowers blooming and trees in leaf, I supposed the inn would be a pretty place, quaint and welcoming. But on a moonlit January night it had a grim, forbidding appearance. Despite the warm air from the car's heater, I shivered. No wonder Gina said it was haunted. If I were a stranger looking for a place to stay I'd drive on, hoping to find a nice modern motel in the next town.

"Isn't it lovely?" Dad asked fondly. "Susan and I are so happy here. It's the sort of home we've always wanted."

"It's very picturesque," I said, choosing my words carefully.

"Yes," Dad said, "that's just what our guests say." Shifting into second gear, he drove slowly downhill toward the inn. A woman stood on the stone steps, waving to us. At her side was a little boy. The moment the car stopped, he ran to meet us.

"Daddy! Daddy!" he shouted. "Did you bring her?"

Dad gestured to me. "Todd, this is Cynda. Cynda, this is Todd."

My half brother gave me a quick, shy smile. When Dad picked him up for a kiss, I felt the sharp bite of jealousy. I turned away, only to stumble into Susan's outstretched arms. Giving me a hug, she led me into a spacious entry hall.

13

"I'm so glad you're here," she began. "You can't believe how lonesome I've been for company this winter. Todd's marvelous, but he's not much of a conversationalist yet."

Despite the warmth of her greeting, I hung back, tense and unsure of myself. Susan was young, no more than twenty-seven or -eight, and prettier than the pictures I'd seen. As rosy as I was pale, she wore her thick, tawny hair pulled back in a long, loose braid, emphasizing her cheekbones and short, straight nose.

She was also just pregnant enough to show—a fact my father had neglected to mention.

Still holding Todd, Dad put one arm around Susan. "We'd have been here sooner," he said, "but we stopped at the diner for a quick break. I hope you weren't worried, Susie."

After giving Dad a kiss to show she forgave him, Susan took my jacket and pointed out the bathroom. "If I know Jeff, you probably drank a zillion cups of coffee."

I locked the door and leaned against it, grateful for an opportunity to be alone for a few minutes. I needed a chance to relax, gather my thoughts, get used to being in a strange place with people I didn't know.

Susan said something, and Dad laughed. I felt like an eavesdropper hiding in the bathroom. A spy, an outsider. A loud banging on the door startled me. "What are you doing in there?" Todd shouted. "There's cake and cookies and all kinds of good stuff. Nobody can have any till you come out!"

14

"Don't be rude, Todd," Susan said sharply. "Cynda will join us when she's ready."

Mortified, I opened the door and tried to return Todd's smile.

"This way," he said, taking my hand and leading me into the living room.

A fire crackled on the hearth. Instead of turning on the lamps, Susan had lit dozens of candles; they glowed on the ornately carved wood mantel, on tables laden with books and pottery, and in deep window recesses where the flames danced in the small panes, multiplied many times over.

In the dim light, I made out two walls of floor-to-ceiling bookcases, framed paintings and photographs, and a small winged statue on a pedestal. In one corner a moon-faced grandfather's clock ticked solemnly. In another, a black carousel horse threw back its head in a toothy grin.

I took a seat near the fire in an old armchair shaped by generations of backs. Never had I seen a room as cozy and intimate as this. Mom and Steve were minimalists when it came to interior decoration. We lived in a modern glass box, austere and strictly functional. Nothing to catch dust. At Underhill, dust seemed to be part of the decor.

Above the snap and pop of the fire, the wind howled, prowling around the inn, snooping at the windows and whining at the door. The candle flames quivered in the draft, melting the wax into strange shapes.

"You must think your father has brought you to

15

the back of the north wind." Susan smiled at me over the rim of her teacup. "Trust me, everything will look better in the morning."

While his mother talked, Todd snuggled into the chair beside me. "Will you read me a story, Cynda? Not a scary one, I get bad dreams."

Susan shook her head. "Not tonight, Todd. It's already way past your bedtime. You stayed up late to see Cynda, remember?"

Todd ignored his mother. "Do you ever have bad dreams, Cynda?"

"Sometimes," I said, suddenly aware of the darkness beyond the candlelight, the empty rooms, the creaking floors.

"My dreams are about wolves," Todd whispered. "I wake up and I think a wolf is under my bed or in the closet. I make Daddy and Mommy look in all the dark places to make sure he isn't hiding somewhere, waiting to eat me up. They don't believe he's real, but—"

"Now, Todd," Dad interrupted, "let's not get started on wolves. You'll keep us up all night."

Susan took his hand. "Time for bed, Toddy."

He looked at his mother pleadingly. "No, not yet, Mommy. I want to talk to Cynda."

Dad shook his head. "Cynda's tired and so are you, Todd. You can talk tomorrow."

Todd began to cry, further proof he was tired, Dad said. Susan led him upstairs, but he protested every step of the way. From somewhere above, I heard him wailing about the wolf.

16

Dad sighed. "You were just like him when you were five. Imagining monsters in the closet, witches under your bed, wolves behind the door. You grew out of it, and I'm sure Todd will too. Hopefully before he turns sixteen."

I leaned my head against the back of the chair, glad Dad remembered my childhood. Sometimes the years he'd lived with Mom and me seemed as unreal as a good dream you can't quite recall in the morning.

Dad caught me yawning. Picking up my suitcases, he led me down the hall, past the dining room and the kitchen, all the way to the back of the inn.

"Susan, Todd, and I sleep on the third floor," he said. "The second floor's for guests—six rooms, empty at the moment and likely to stay that way till spring."

He opened a heavy wooden door and stood back to let me enter first. "This is the oldest part of the inn. It was originally the kitchen, but when we renovated we made it into a big bedroom with a private bath. Susan and I thought you'd enjoy having the best Underhill has to offer."

I walked around the room—my room, the one Dad had chosen for me. The floor was brick and slightly uneven. Thick wool carpets, woven in intricate patterns, covered most of it. Overhead, the rough-hewn rafters were black with age. Among the furnishings were a table and chair, a massive wardrobe carved with strange animal faces and foliage, a matching chest, and a high, canopied bed.

As in the living room, the walls were lined with shelves of books. At one end was a fireplace tall enough to walk into. Electric candles shone in the windows, and a space heater glowed on the hearth.

Dad gestured at the big black cat sleeping on the bed. "If you don't want Ebony to stay, I'll take him with me."

At the sound of his name, Ebony opened his eyes a slit, glanced at me, twitched his tail idly, and went back to sleep.

I leaned over the bed to stroke him. "He's beautiful," I said quickly. "He can sleep here every single night."

Dad showed me how the heater worked, demonstrated the high-tech shower in the bathroom, and finally gave me a hug and a good-night kiss. "It's nice to have you here, Cynda," he said. "Sleep well."

After he left, the room didn't seem quite as cozy. To keep from thinking scary thoughts, I busied myself unpacking. It made me feel more at home to see my shampoo and conditioner in the shower caddy, my hair dryer, brush, and comb on the shelf above the washbasin, my soap in the soap dish.

After I'd washed my face and brushed my teeth, I hung my clothes in the closet and put my underwear in the tall chest near the bed. Last of all, I made room on the nightstand for a picture of Mom.

Satisfied the room was now truly mine, I undressed quickly and pulled on my warmest nightgown. Safe in bed, I turned off the lamp, leaving the electric candles burning on the windowsill. It was strange how the flick of a switch altered things. Shadows ate up the furniture and filled the corners. The candles' dim light illuminated a picture here, a mirror there. The faces carved on the wardrobe looked more grotesque, even sinister.

Outside the wind continued to howl. A branch rapped the glass over and over again, *tappity tappity tappity*. Far away, an owl hooted once, twice, three times.

I reached for Ebony and drew him closer. He nestled into the curve of my body and began to purr. Despite the eerie creaks and groans of the old building, I fell asleep.

3

Todd woke me in the morning, leaping on the bed and shouting, "Cynda, Cynda, get up! Daddy made pancakes 'specially for you."

I burrowed under the covers, but Todd refused to let me sleep. He continued to jump up and down, shouting about pancakes, bouncing so hard the bed shook. A blue blanket he'd tied around his shoulders ballooned like a cape. His face was flushed, his eyes shone. "You have to do what Captain Jupiter says!"

I glared at him, but it was hard not to laugh. "Leave me alone, you little pest!"

The noise brought Susan to the door. "Toddy, don't bother Cynda. Let her sleep if she wants to."

By the time Susan hauled Todd off the bed, I was wide awake.

"Poor Cynda," Susan said with a smile. "Now you know what it's like to have a little brother."

When they were gone, I dressed quickly. My room was so cold the windowpanes were frosted with ice pictures—flowers, ferns, leaves, and stars so fragile a puff of warm breath could destroy them.

Shivering in the frigid air, I yanked a comb through my hair and ran down the hall to the kitchen. Sunshine poured through the windows and gave a scarlet glow to the potted geraniums on the sills. Beethoven's Sixth Symphony played on the stereo. The air smelled of fresh-brewed coffee, pancakes, and maple syrup. At the table, Dad, Susan, and Todd welcomed me with smiles.

Last night's spooky atmosphere was gone. So was my loneliness. Feeling like part of the family, I took a seat. "Sorry to keep you waiting," I apologized. "You should have started without me."

"That's just what I said," Todd told me, "but Mommy and Daddy made me wait and wait."

Dad looked up from the pile of pancakes he was flooding with syrup. "Don't talk with your mouth full, son. No one wants to see your half-chewed food."

Todd swallowed and opened his mouth wide. "All gone."

"That's better." Dad passed the syrup to me. "Did you sleep well, Cynda?"

At the same time, Susan asked if I'd been warm enough and Todd wanted to know if I'd seen or heard any wolves.

It was Todd's question I answered. "I heard the wind and an owl, but not a single wolf came near the inn all night long."

Todd looked at me solemnly, eyes wide, fork raised halfway to his mouth. "I heard one scratching at my door. He said, 'Little boy, little boy, let me come in.'"

21

Dad leaned toward Todd. "And you said, 'Not by the hair of my chinny-chin-chin.'"

Todd scowled. "It's not funny, Daddy."

Dad laughed. "You've read too many fairy tales, son." He opened the newspaper and began reading, but Todd wasn't ready to give up.

"If a big bad wolf knocked on our door, would you let him in?"

Without raising his head, Dad said, "In real life, a wolf wouldn't want to come into someone's house."

"You can't be sure what wolves want," Todd muttered. "They can be very tricky, Daddy."

Dad rattled the paper and frowned as if he were tired of being interrupted. "Eat your pancakes, Todd. They're getting cold."

I glanced at my brother. Still worried about the wolf, he poked at the pancakes on his plate, his joy in them gone. It seemed to me Dad should have put the paper down and listened to him. Asked more questions. Been more reassuring. Instead he'd scoffed at Todd's fears just as he'd scoffed at Gina's ghost.

I tapped Todd's hand to get his attention. "I bet Captain Jupiter would chase the wolf away," I whispered.

Todd smiled and brandished his fork like a sword. "That's right," he said. "Captain Jupiter would kill the wolf dead."

*

After breakfast, Dad suggested a walk to the ocean, a ten-minute hike from the inn. Despite the cold, I was eager for another opportunity to talk to my father. Perhaps we'd finally find the words to make up for the years we'd lived apart. We'd be together again, truly a father and daughter.

The temperature was five above zero, not counting the wind chill. Dad set out across the snow, expecting me to follow. I stumbled after him, clumsy in high boots but determined to keep up with his long-legged stride. By the time we reached the cliff top, I was beginning to wish I'd stayed home. It was too cold to have the sort of deep conversation I'd planned.

"Isn't the view magnificent?" Dad swept his arm wide, taking in the shore below us, the small islands dotting the ocean, the cloudless blue sky over our heads.

I went as close to the edge as I dared and looked down at the waves pounding the rocks far below. I was horrified to see a body floating in the surf. White dress, pale face, long hair streaming. I clutched Dad's arm and pointed. "There's something in the water, a girl."

"Where?"

The two of us studied the ocean. The body was gone. "She must have sunk," I whispered.

Suddenly a log rose to the surface, trailing white rags and long brown strands of seaweed.

"There's your body," Dad said as a wave carried the log shoreward and then sucked it back.

I watched the log sink and then resurface. "Yes," I said with relief, "yes, that's it."

Dad took my arm. "Come on," he said. "A fall from here could be fatal."

I followed him along a path that twisted and turned down to the shore. Out of the wind at last, we walked along a narrow strip of sand, threading our way between rocks and tidal pools rimmed with fragile ice. Overhead, gulls cried harshly. Waves rolled in, tumbling over each other in their haste to reach land, breaking with crashes like thunder.

I breathed the salty air deep into my lungs, loving the smell and taste of it. I wanted to run and jump and twirl round and round, but I was afraid of looking silly and clumsy, so I made myself walk beside Dad.

When we'd gone at least a couple of miles, we sat on a sun-warmed rock to rest. Dad struggled to light his pipe, and I poked at stones half buried in the sand, levering them out one by one with a stick. Every now and then, I glanced at Dad, hoping he might want to talk, but he was staring out to sea, puffing on his pipe, apparently content to say nothing.

Afraid to interrupt his thoughts, I added shells and driftwood to my pile of stones, thinking I'd take them back to my room and make a still life. They had an interesting Andrew Wyeth look, bleached and dry as artifacts from an ancient tomb.

Finally Dad turned to me. "We need to talk about your education, Cynda."

I continued poking at a particularly interesting green rock, just the right size and shape to be a

24

dinosaur egg. Education wasn't what I'd hoped to discuss. Without looking up, I said, "What about it?"

"Rockpoint High School is more than an hour's drive from here," Dad said. "Considering winter road conditions, I set up a home-study program for you. If you apply yourself, you can finish your junior year ahead of time." That sounded fine with me.

While Dad talked about the books he'd ordered, I watched the waves wash in and out, leaving messages from the sea—a scalloped fringe of seaweed studded with broken shells and bits of wood, an old bleach bottle, a soda can, a dead crab sprawled on its back and looking like the bones of a dead man's hand.

"Here's the schedule," Dad was saying. "A study session from nine till twelve, an hour for lunch, another study session till three or so."

"That takes care of most of the day," I said.

"It takes discipline to work at home," Dad went on, missing my sarcasm. "You have to be a tough boss if you hope to accomplish anything."

With that, he stood up, brushed the sand off his pants, and said, "My stomach tells me it's lunchtime."

I dropped my stones into my pocket and trudged along beside Dad. On the way back to the inn, he named the birds swooping and soaring over our heads. Black-backed gulls, ring-billed gulls, Iceland gulls, black-legged kittiwakes, Wilson's storm petrels —the great naturalist knew them all. I listened dutifully, but it seemed to me Dad was deliberately holding me at arm's length, leaving no openings for intimate conversation.

When we were halfway to the cliff path, I was disappointed to see Susan strolling toward us, her long hair streaming in the wind. Todd ran ahead, crying our names. I hung back, wishing Dad would slow down too. Once Todd and Susan joined us, I'd have to share my father again, no closer to him than I'd been before we left the inn.

"Cynda, Daddy, look at me, look at me!" Todd scrambled to the top of a boulder, his cape fluttering in the wind, and waved a wooden sword. When he was sure he had our attention, he cried, "Captain Jupiter to the rescue!" and jumped, landing with a thump on the hard sand.

Dad lifted Todd over his head and settled him on his shoulders. Susan reached for Dad's hand, uniting the three of them. I trudged along behind, picking up stones and dropping them into my pockets, deliberately letting a gap open between us. As it widened, their voices grew fainter. The cries of gulls and the roar of waves came between us.

It was childish but I wondered how long it would take them to notice how far away I was. When would they miss me, look back, call out to me?

At last, Todd turned and waved his sword. "Cynda," he shouted. "Cynda, hurry up!"

Hands still clasped, Dad and Susan waited for me. I walked slowly toward them, my pockets heavy with stones.

4

Not long after lunch, someone rapped on the kitchen door. "That must be Mrs. Bigelow," Susan said as Todd ran to let in a ruddy-faced little woman.

"Lord, it's cold," she said, shedding her coat and scarf. "From the way it's clouding up, we're bound to have snow tonight."

Turning to me with a smile, she introduced herself. "You must be Cynda. My friend Gina told me she met you last night at the diner."

She gave my hand a friendly squeeze and turned back to Susan. "I'd best be about my work. I don't want Will fetching me after dark. If I'm right about the snow, the roads will be bad."

After Mrs. Bigelow scurried upstairs to clean, I lingered at the table, sipping tea. I'd had little to say during lunch, but nobody noticed because Todd entertained us with endless knock-knock jokes, most of which he'd invented himself and made no sense to anyone but him. Susan and Dad laughed anyway which inspired him to even greater heights of silliness.

Long before I finished my tea, Susan excused herself and went to her sewing room. Todd tagged along with her. Dad disappeared into his den to write, leaving me with no one to talk to.

Bored, I went to the living room and picked up one of Dad's mysteries. I'd never read any of his books. Mom had given me the idea they were poorly written and plotted. Violent, too. Filled with bad language and sex. She said I'd be embarrassed to admit Dad was my father.

I made myself comfortable and opened *Dead but Not Forgotten*, an Inspector Marathon mystery by the author of *The Cruel Hereafter*, Dad's most popular book. Although it wasn't great literature, the novel was a lot better than Mom claimed.

After several chapters, I was distracted by the rumble of the vacuum cleaner. Remembering what Gina had said about Mrs. Bigelow, I laid Dad's book aside. I'd promised myself to ask her about the ghost when she came to clean the inn. She was upstairs right now. Maybe she'd stop working long enough to tell me exactly what she'd experienced.

I left the living room quietly and followed the sound of the vacuum cleaner to a guest room on the second floor. Mrs. Bigelow was by herself, hard at work. When she saw me in the doorway, she gasped and pressed her hand to her heart.

"My goodness, Cynda, you gave me a fright. I didn't hear you coming." Switching off the vacuum cleaner, she laughed. "I get jumpy up here all by myself."

"The inn's a spooky old place," I agreed, "especially at night."

Mrs. Bigelow fidgeted with the switch on the vacuum cleaner, as if she weren't sure whether to continue working or stop and talk. "Gina told me she spoke to you and your father about the ghost," she began hesitantly. "I hope she didn't frighten you, Cynda."

"I wasn't scared," I said quickly. "Just curious. I wanted to hear more, but Dad kept insisting it was all nonsense. He doesn't believe in things like that, you know, but I—well, I was hoping you'd tell me about the ghost. If that's what it is."

"Oh, that's what it is, all right." Mrs. Bigelow sighed and sat on the edge of the bed. I perched beside her. The room was gauzy with shadows, the air still and cold. I wished I'd worn a warmer sweater.

"I guess you ought to know," Mrs. Bigelow went on. "After all, it's no secret, though I doubt the real estate agent told your father. Mr. Hunnicott was so anxious to get Underhill off his hands, he didn't want to say anything that might get in the way of the deal."

Mrs. Bigelow paused as if she were searching for the right words. Trying hard to be patient, I waited while she gnawed her lip and thought. Finally she looked at me. "A girl was murdered near here sixty or seventy years ago. My father was one of the fishermen who found her at the bottom of the cliff. A terrible sight, he said. Remembered it till the day he died."

She reached for my hand and squeezed it. "She'd been in the water so long there wasn't a drop of blood in her body, but it was clear someone had slashed her

29

throat and thrown her into the sea. Like a snow maiden she was, washed pure by the salt water."

I stared at Mrs. Bigelow, chilled through and through by the memory of what I thought I'd seen in the ocean. "Why would anybody do something like that?" I whispered.

She shook her head sadly. "No one knows, Cynda. The last time the girl was seen alive, she was walking on the cliffs with a man. The police searched for months, they questioned people for miles around, but it was as if the earth had swallowed him up. They never found him."

I gazed into the shadows darkening the corners. The sky had clouded over since lunch and the short winter day was sinking into dull, gray dusk. "Why does she haunt the inn?" I asked.

Mrs. Bigelow tightened her grip on my hand. "She used to live here, Cynda. This was her home. It's the only place the poor, lost creature knows."

"Have you ever seen her?"

"Not seen, no, but sometimes she comes close enough to touch, close enough to feel—if spirits could be touched or felt. Sad she is and cold, so cold the hair on my arms rises when she's near."

Mrs. Bigelow drew back. "Lord, look at you. You're as white as a ghost yourself. Oh, my, I've gone and scared you half to death."

"No, it's all right, I'm fine," I protested, but I couldn't stop shivering. "I'd better go now. I promised Todd I'd read to him this afternoon."

Mrs. Bigelow looked at me closely. "You've got

nothing to fear from her, Cynda. It's her killer she seeks, but he's dead and buried himself now. That's why she can't rest. Her death was never avenged, her killer was never brought to justice."

By the time Mrs. Bigelow finished that last sentence, I'd backed away to the door. "Like the ghost of Hamlet's father," I whispered. "'Doomed for a certain time to walk the night . . .'"

I don't think Mrs. Bigelow heard me. She'd turned away, her hand on the vacuum cleaner, ready to resume her work.

Without looking back, I fled downstairs. Behind me, the vacuum cleaner roared into life, but even that familiar sound couldn't calm my nerves.

*

A few minutes later, Todd found me at the living room window watching snowflakes the size of duck feathers swirl down from the clouds. I was thinking about the dead girl. Once she'd stood where I stood now, seeing what I saw now. Snow in winter, green fields in summer, moonlight and sunlight, blue skies and gray, dawn and dusk. Like me, she'd run up and down the inn's stairs; she'd warmed herself at the fire; she'd laughed, she'd cried; she'd gone in and out, always expecting to return.

Todd tugged my arm to get my attention. "Where have you been, Cynda? You promised to read to me. Remember?"

I took the books he handed me, glad for something to keep me from thinking about death and dying.

31

Halfway through the second story, Todd was distracted by the sound of a truck laboring up the driveway to the inn. Twisting around, he peered out the window.

"It's Will!" he cried happily.

Jumping off the couch, he ran into the kitchen and opened the back door. "Will, Will, come in!" I heard him shout.

While I was putting the books away, Todd returned. To my surprise, he dragged a boy into the living room with him. I'd expected Will to be Mrs. Bigelow's husband, but I'd obviously made a mistake. The boy was about my age, too young to be Mrs. Bigelow's son, let alone her husband.

"This is my new big sister, Cynda," Todd said proudly. "I told you she was coming to live with us. And—ta-dah—here she is."

Will smiled. He was tall and thin, curly-haired, and rosy-cheeked from the cold. Not exactly handsome, at least not in the way movie stars are. His face was too narrow, his mouth too wide. But he was good-looking enough to make me wish I'd spent more time on my hair.

"I came to pick up my grandmother," Will said. "Is she ready to leave?"

The vacuum cleaner was roaring overhead. "It sounds like she's still cleaning," I said, glad Will didn't know it was my fault Mrs. Bigelow wasn't finished yet.

We stared at each other. As usual, I couldn't think

of anything to say, clever or otherwise. Apparently Will was as inept at making conversation as I was. He shifted his weight from one foot to the other. I brushed at a speck of lint on my sweater sleeve. The hall clock chimed the half hour. The vacuum cleaner droned.

Todd tugged at Will's hand. "Come see my castle. It's got two knights, a dragon, and a drawbridge. Daddy helped, but I built most of it."

Will glanced at me as Todd towed him toward the kitchen. "If you need a ride to school, I can take you," he said suddenly. "My truck's not much but it's better than being stuck on the bus for a couple of hours."

"Thanks," I said, following him and Todd. "But Dad set up a home-study program for me."

"Lucky you," Will said.

Todd interrupted before he could say more. Thrusting a plastic knight into Will's hand, he said, "You guard the north gate and I'll guard the south gate. Whatever you do, don't let the wolf in."

"What wolf?" Will asked.

Todd handed me a small rubber wolf. "Cynda, you be the wolf."

"What if I don't want to?" I laid the wolf down, resenting the way Todd thrust himself into the center of everything. I wanted to talk to Will, not play a dumb game.

Todd stared at me, obviously surprised. "We can't play if you won't be the wolf."

"Sorry," I said. Getting to my feet, I left the kitchen, thinking Will would follow me. Surely he didn't want to play with a five-year-old.

But I was wrong. Behind me, I heard Will say, "Don't cry, Todd. I'll be the wolf *and* the guard."

I flung myself down on the couch. Except for the electric candles on the window sill, the living room was dark. I could have turned on a light, but I didn't. The dark suited my mood.

In the kitchen, Todd shouted, "Bad wolf!" and Will laughed. Now that it was too late, I wished I'd taken the wolf and played Todd's silly game. I hadn't expected Will to go along with my brother. I'd misjudged the situation.

Which wasn't unusual. I always had trouble making friends, especially boyfriends. I'd been in love dozens of times, but it was always the unrequited kind. I'd fall for a boy because his eyes were the color of fog or his smile was as warm as candlelight or his laugh reminded me of sleighbells at Christmas. I'd worship him from across the library or the football field and then watch him fall in love with somebody else—a cheerleader or a gymnast or the star of the class play.

Maybe it was because I was shy and didn't know how to smile and flirt and make boys comfortable. Maybe it was because I wasn't pretty enough. Or sexy. Maybe it was because we moved so often. Whatever the reason, I stumbled over everything from words to my big pair of left feet.

Suddenly a light went on, nearly blinding me. "My

34

goodness, Cynda, what are you doing sitting here all by yourself in the dark?" Mrs. Bigelow asked.

Before I could answer, Todd ran into the room. Flinging his arms around Mrs. Bigelow, he cried, "Please let Will stay a little longer. He promised to draw me a picture."

My little brother's charms didn't work on Mrs. Bigelow. Shaking her head, she said, "It's snowing, dear. You know how steep the road to our place is. You wouldn't want us to get stuck, would you?"

With that, Mrs. Bigelow went to the kitchen to fetch her coat and scarf. Todd and I trailed along behind her.

While Will helped his grandmother bundle up, Todd bombarded him with questions. "Are you going to plow our driveway tomorrow? Can I help? Can I ride in the truck with you?"

Will grinned and shrugged. "We'll see, Todd, we'll see."

Todd scowled. "Dumbhead, you sound just like Daddy!"

Susan looked up from the pie she was making for dessert. "Don't be fresh, Todd."

"Come on, Will," Mrs. Bigelow urged. "The snow's coming down harder and harder."

Will lingered for a second in the doorway. "It was nice meeting you, Cynda. I'll probably be back tomorrow afternoon with the plow. See you then."

I smiled at Will, pleased he'd made a special point of saying goodbye to me. Maybe my refusal to play Todd's game hadn't made me look as bad as I'd

35

feared. Maybe Will liked me after all. Or maybe he was just being polite. He was so nice it was hard to tell.

After the Bigelows left, I retreated to my room to escape the noise Todd was making with his blocks. I intended to read for a while before dinner, but it was hard to concentrate. The clock ticked loudly. The wind rose. Snow hissed against the windows. Tree limbs rattled like dry bones.

I thought of the dead girl, her face as white as seafoam, her hair floating on the waves—a sight so terrible that Mrs. Bigelow's father remembered it till his dying day. Murdered—she was murdered and thrown into the ocean. And her killer was never caught.

I searched the shadows fearfully, looking and listening for signs of the girl's presence. I saw nothing, heard nothing, but I was sure she was nearby, watching me.

With all my coward's heart, I wished I'd never gone upstairs, never pestered Mrs. Bigelow, never learned about the dead girl.

5

Since he'd opened Underhill, Dad had become a gourmet cook. He took great pride in preparing my first dinner at Underhill—a lavish spread of Maine food, including lobster and clams and fancy little potatoes, topped off with Susan's deep-dish apple pie.

After we'd eaten, Dad took Todd to bed. While we waited for him to return, Susan busied herself fixing tea. The kitchen was warm and cozy, but outside, Mrs. Bigelow's snow had become a howling blizzard.

Susan turned to me. "Isn't Will nice, Cynda?"

Trying to sound indifferent, I shrugged and said, "He's okay, I guess."

I'd been daydreaming about Will all evening, but I didn't want Susan to know. More than likely, he already had a girlfriend. Even if he didn't, I doubted he'd be interested in me. It looked like another case of unrequited love was looming on my horizon.

"Things haven't been easy for Will," Susan went on. "He came here from Boston four or five years ago. Some problem with his parents. A divorce, I guess."

While Susan talked, I studied a poster on the wall behind her, pictures of vegetables labeled with their French names. Potato: *pomme de terre*; bean: *haricot*; onion: *oignon*; garlic: *ail*. I mouthed the words silently, trying to get the pronunciation right, but I was listening to everything Susan said.

"The kids around here don't accept outsiders easily, so he's become something of a loner," she was saying. "It worries Mrs. Bigelow that he's made so few friends, but he seems happy enough to me."

"Are you talking about Will?" Dad strolled into the kitchen and dropped his long frame into a chair. "It's his artistic temperament, Susie. He'd be a loner no matter where he lived."

Tilting back, he balanced precariously on two chair legs and smiled at me. "Ask him to show you his paintings someday, Cynda. The boy has real talent."

Susan poured a cup of tea for Dad. "You were upstairs a long time, Jeff. Was Todd more difficult than usual?"

"No matter how many books I read, he begged for another. Then it was a song, then a glass of water, then a search under the bed for wolves. He's wearing me out."

Susan patted Dad's shoulder. "Poor old Papa," she joked.

Dad laughed and pressed his ear against her stomach. "Lord, Susie," he murmured, "it's kicking up a storm already."

I turned away, wishing Dad would save that kind

of thing for later. Mom and Steve were just as bad. Always hugging and kissing, never realizing they were making me uncomfortable.

Releasing Susan, Dad said, "You know what I think the problem is? Todd's worried about the baby."

"But we've talked to him about it so often, Jeff. Surely he knows it won't change our love for him."

For a few minutes, I listened to Dad and Susan discuss Todd's insecurities, but the conversation soon began to annoy me. Todd, Todd, Todd—present or absent, my half brother dominated the household. In my opinion, it wouldn't hurt him to have a rival. I had to share Dad. Why shouldn't Todd do the same with a younger child?

Finally I said I was going to bed. I hoped Dad would realize he'd been ignoring me and apologize. Instead, Susan yawned. She was tired too. Taking Dad's hand, she led him into the hall, turning back once to ask if I'd mind rinsing the cups and saucers before I turned in.

I slung the dishes into the sink, making as much noise as I could, but I doubt if either Dad or Susan heard me. The inn was too big, its walls too thick for sounds to carry all the way to the third floor.

Ebony stalked into the kitchen and brushed against my legs, probably hoping I'd feed him. To keep him interested, I poured a little milk into a bowl. "See this? If you want it, you have to come with me."

My little ploy worked. Ebony followed me down the dark hall, almost tripping me in his eagerness to get the milk. Once we were in my room, I shut the door to make sure he stayed. I didn't want to be alone. Not with a ghost prowling the inn.

I undressed quickly and got into bed, thinking Ebony would curl up beside me. Instead he leaped to the windowsill. When I called him, he ignored me. So much for feline gratitude.

"All right," I muttered. "If you won't come to me, I'll come to you."

I slid out of bed, determined to make the cat do what I wanted. Always a mistake. When I tried to pick him up, he growled softly—not at me but at something outside.

I peered through the glass, trying to see what Ebony saw. Snow fell thick and fast, obscuring most of the view, but I thought I heard the mutter of an engine. Slowly a sleek, silver car emerged from a veil of snow as white and pure as a bride's.

It was a terrible night to be out, far from shelter and alone. "Stop," I whispered, taking pity on the driver. "Come in from the cold, stay with us."

The car hesitated as if the driver heard my invitation and wanted to accept, but drifts blocked the inn's entrance, making it impossible. After a moment, the car's headlights flashed off and on. Then I watched as its taillights vanished, glowing like red eyes in the swirling snow.

An icy draft eddied around my ankles, but I stayed at the window, staring into the darkness. What sort of person ventured out on a night like this? Where was he going? As far as I knew, the road led to the sea and then followed the coast to Blue Port, a town even smaller than Ferrington.

I took a deep, shivery breath and went back to bed. It made no sense, but I knew I'd see that car again. Maybe not tonight, maybe not till after the storm, but someday it would return to Underhill. That eerie certainty kept me awake for at least an hour, listening for the purr of the engine.

*

It was still snowing when I woke up. By the time it stopped that afternoon, we'd gotten at least two feet, maybe three. The weather report called it the storm of the century, the worst in years. Fences and roads, hedges, bushes, and rocks—everything was buried except the trees.

The blizzard's ferocity made me doubt I'd really seen a car pass the inn. Nothing could have gotten through that snow. Yet the anticipation I'd felt last night persisted. The sleek, silver car would return. I sensed it coming the way some people sense thunderstorms or earthquakes.

My strange mood made me nervous and restless. Impatient. Irritable. I accused Todd of cheating when we played Candyland. As bad-tempered as I, he knocked down a block castle I'd spent an hour building. I called him a spoiled brat, he pulled my hair. I threatened to slap him, he told Susan. She got cross and blamed everything on me.

When Will showed up to plow and shovel, Dad ordered us to go outside. "I need some peace and

41

quiet," he shouted. "How can I finish this novel with all the noise you're making?"

When Todd began to cry, Dad must have realized how cross he'd sounded. Giving Todd a hug, he apologized to both of us. "I don't know what got into me. I've been edgy all morning."

Todd was the first to recover. Pulling me toward the coat closet, he begged me to help him with his boots, his jacket zipper, and his mittens.

By the time the two of us were ready to face the cold, Will had finished plowing and was hard at work shoveling the walk. The wind had reddened his nose and cheeks, making his eyes even bluer.

Todd ran in circles around him, grabbing for the shovel. "Let me help," he shouted. "I'm five now, I'm strong, I can do it!"

Will stuck the shovel in a snowbank and grinned. "Too late, Todd. I'm already done."

"Let's make angels then." Todd dragged Will across the lawn and fell flat on his back, pulling Will down with him. "Come on, Cynda," he shouted. "Make an angel next to mine. They can be brother and sister, just like you and me."

I'd been hanging back, too shy to join in Todd's antics till someone invited me. Preferably Will. But he hadn't really looked at me, hadn't spoken to me either.

Will saw me hesitating and jumped to his feet. I didn't notice the snowball in his hand until he threatened to throw it. "You heard Todd," he said, laughing. "Get over here, Cynda."

42

I didn't want to repeat the mistake I'd made with the wolf game. Nor did I want to be hit with a snowball. Before Will had a chance to aim at me, I ran across the snow and flopped down beside Todd. Imitating him and Will, I swished my arms and legs to make the angel's wings and skirt.

We scrambled to our feet to admire the three angels. Todd grabbed my hand. "Aren't they pretty, Cynda?"

I stared at my half brother. His eyes were clear and blue, his cheeks were pink, his knit cap had fallen off to expose a tangle of blond curls. Except for his hair, he looked just like a picture of me taken on a snowy day when I was five. Mom and Dad had been married then, we'd lived in a big, old house in Albany, and I'd thought Dad was mine for keeps. Like Todd, I'd been trustful and happy, eager to please, eager to be loved.

Suddenly I wanted to keep Todd safe, I wanted him to stay happy. I wanted him to love me, I wanted to love him. Fighting an urge to cry, I said, "They're the prettiest angels I ever saw, Toddy."

He laughed and turned to Will. "Now for the snowman!"

Will winked at me. "Yes, sir!" he said. "When Captain Jupiter speaks, we underlings must obey."

We worked on the snowman for more than an hour. By the time we were finished, he was over six feet tall and very dapper in an old fedora and a plaid scarf. Will had given him a melancholy face and Todd had cajoled Dad into contributing a pipe and a worn-

43

out pair of shoes. The snowman looked capable of strolling off to Ferrington for a cup of coffee at the diner or coming to the inn for a night's lodging.

Just before sunset, Susan called us inside for hot chocolate and fresh-baked peanut butter cookies. Will and I raced each other to the door, laughing and shoving like kids. Todd ran after us and flung himself at me, knocking me into a snow-covered bush. Will hauled me out, and, still laughing, we burst into the warm kitchen.

Shedding layers of coats, gloves, scarves, and hats, we set our snow-filled boots near the wood stove to dry and gathered around the table. My toes and fingers throbbed with cold, my teeth ached, even my forehead hurt, but I was having too much fun to care. For once, I seemed to be saying and doing the right things. I didn't feel tense or anxious, I wasn't worried about anything. I was actually happy.

When nothing was left of the cookies but crumbs, Todd handed Will a pencil and a piece of paper. "Draw Captain Jupiter killing a wolf," he said. "Show the wolf dead. Make the snow red with his blood."

Will glanced at me. "Where does Todd get his ideas?"

"Have you ever read any of my father's mysteries?"

He grinned. "I guess it runs in the family."

Todd nudged Will's hand. "Shut up and draw," he said. "Captain Jupiter commands you."

"Yes, sir." Will picked up the pencil and began. Todd watched closely, offering suggestions. I don't know what I'd expected—cartoon figures maybe, stiff and stylized the way boys often draw, but Will brought Captain Jupiter to life. His cape swung as he stood over the dead wolf, gripping a sword in both hands, his face grim and determined.

I leaned close to watch Will add background details—bare trees, snow, the full moon. "I wish I could draw like that."

He looked up, his face inches from mine, and smiled as if I'd genuinely pleased him. "Drawing's the only thing I'm good at," he said. "It's what I want to do for the rest of my life."

Signing his name with a grand flourish, Will leaned back in his chair. He was wearing a patterned sweater, knitted in shades of blue that complimented his eyes. Mrs. Bigelow's handiwork, I thought. Thick and soft, it had the kind of texture you wanted to touch.

"Draw another one," Todd said.

"Next time," Will said, getting to his feet. "It's past six. Grandmother worries if I'm late."

Todd followed him to the door, begging him to come back soon, making him promise to draw more pictures. "A shark, a dinosaur, a dragon—Captain Jupiter can kill them all."

Before he escaped, Will grinned at me. "Maybe I'll draw something for you, too, Cynda."

The minute the door shut, Todd ran to the window and watched Will drive away. When the last rumble of the truck's engine faded into the night, he

45

turned to me. "Look at our snowman, Cynda. He's so lonesome out there. I wish he could come inside with us."

I peered over Todd's shoulder. The snowman's hat shadowed his face, giving him a slightly sinister appearance. "I think he likes the cold, Toddy. It's where he belongs."

Todd leaned against me. "But we belong in here, Cynda, where it's all warm and nice and dinner's cooking."

I gave him a quick, shy hug. It was one of those moments you wish you could save forever. The kind of memory you can warm your hands with later when things go wrong.

6

At dinner, my good mood leaked away like air from a tired balloon. I grew increasingly nervous, anxious, worried. Even though Dad's stuffed flounder was delicious, I couldn't eat more than a mouthful or two. If anyone had spoken harshly to me, I would have cried.

Todd was edgy too. He wiggled and whined. Let his nose run without wiping it. Sneezed without covering his mouth. Played with his food and said he wasn't hungry. When he called me a dummy, Dad turned to him crossly. "What have I told you about that word? No one's dumb, son. No one's a dummy."

Susan nodded in agreement. "Eat your dinner, Todd."

He scowled at his flounder. "Why did you put this icky, lumpy junk on it? You know I like mine plain."

Susan sighed and began to clear the table. "Somebody's awfully cranky," she murmured as she took Todd's plate. "Maybe we need to go to bed early."

Todd jutted his lip out, but before he could protest, the doorbell chimed.

Susan stared at Dad. "Who on earth can that be?"

Dad got to his feet, and Todd ran after him, shouting, "Maybe it's Will!"

Susan looked at me wearily. "Please get him, Cynda. He's been sniffling since he came inside. I don't want him in a draft."

I ran into the hall, eager to see who'd come calling. Like Todd, I hoped it was Will. If he came over in the evening, he might invite me to a movie. Maybe we'd go on a moonlight sled ride, maybe, maybe, maybe . . .

But it wasn't Will. A stranger stood on the porch. The light shone full on his face, shadowing his eyes but accentuating his pale skin and high cheekbones. Sparkles of windblown snow clung to his dark hair and black overcoat. Even though he was at least thirty, he was the handsomest man I'd ever seen, the sort you stop and stare at in disbelief.

"I noticed the candles in your windows," he said. "Am I correct in assuming your inn has a vacancy?"

His voice was deep and rich, colored with a faint accent. British, I thought. With that accent, anything he said, even the tritest phrase, would sound beautiful and fresh and new, as if no one had ever spoken it before.

"Come in, come in." Dad stood back, gesturing graciously. "We have six empty rooms to choose from."

The man glanced at me and I nodded in dumb agreement. It was a cold night, and he was welcome.

He stepped over the threshold, bringing the wintry night inside with him.

Susan hurried down the hall. "For heaven's sake, close the door, Jeff. Can't you feel the draft?"

"Susan, this is Mister—"

"Morthanos," the stranger said softly. "Vincent Morthanos."

Dad shook Mr. Morthanos's hand. "I'm Jeff Bennett. This is my wife Susan, my son Todd, my daughter Cynda."

Mr. Morthanos nodded to each of us, but his eyes lingered on me. "I'm very pleased to meet you," he murmured, extending his hand to Susan, then to me.

His fingers were cold, his grip strong. When he released my hand, I edged closer to Dad, uncertain of my emotions. I wanted to run and hide, yet I wanted to come closer. It was like meeting a movie star I'd adored for years—only I'd never seen Mr. Morthanos before.

Struck dumb, I watched him turn his dark eyes on Todd. "Did you and your big sister build the handsome snowman on the lawn?"

Instead of answering, Todd scowled at Mr. Morthanos. Shrinking from the hand touching his curls, he ran to the kitchen.

"Todd's coming down with a cold," Susan apologized. "I'm afraid it's made him a little out of sorts tonight."

Mr. Morthanos shrugged as if he were accustomed to cranky children. "I quite understand."

"Once Todd's feeling better, you won't be able to get rid of him," Dad said. "He'll be pestering you to read stories or play in the snow—just ask Cynda."

Mr. Morthanos favored me with a charming smile and followed Dad up the stairs to the second floor. Even after they disappeared, I lingered in the hall, listening to the murmur of their voices.

"Mr. Morthanos," I whispered, "Vincent Morthanos." The sound of his name was dark and sweet in my mouth, richer than the richest chocolate.

When Susan called me, I went to the kitchen like someone in a dream, unaware of anything but Mr. Morthanos's footsteps overhead.

Todd looked up from the picture he was coloring. "Cynda, tell Mommy Mr. Morthanos can't stay here. I hate him. Don't you hate him too?"

His outburst took me by surprise. "We don't even know Mr. Morthanos. Why should we hate him?"

Todd made a face. "His fingers are as cold as ice."

"That's not surprising," Susan said. "It must be twenty below tonight."

Rebuked by his mother's frown, Todd lowered his head. In the silence, pellets of windblown snow whispered against the windowpane.

I patted Todd's shoulder, hoping to cheer him up. "Mr. Morthanos loves our snowman."

"He just said that to make me like him." Todd scowled. "Which I don't and won't no matter what he says or does. You mustn't like him either, Cynda!"

Susan sighed. "That's the way it is, Cynda. Todd

either loves you or hates you. With him there's no in-between."

Turning to Todd, she said, "Mr. Morthanos will be here for one night. Surely you can put up with him that long."

But Susan was wrong. When Dad came downstairs, he told us Mr. Morthanos had chosen a room and planned to stay with us for at least a month, maybe longer.

I was thrilled at the prospect of having such a fascinating guest, but Todd howled in protest.

Susan looked at Dad, clearly surprised. "What's the man going to do with himself all day? Everything's closed for the winter, the roads are bad and will probably get worse if we have more snow—"

"Don't worry," Dad interrupted. "All Vincent wants is peace and quiet, time to read and study and work on a book." He smiled. "Poor Susie—it looks like you have two writers in the house now."

"Winter's my chance to take it easy," Susan persisted. "To work on my sewing. Now I'll have a stranger underfoot all day, wanting meals and—"

Dad interrupted again. "We need the money, Susan. The way this book is going, I may never get the second half of my advance. And don't forget who's coming." He smiled and patted Susan's stomach.

Susan sighed. "A couple of nights would be fine, but a month or more . . ." Leaving her sentence unfinished, she turned to Todd, who was kicking the table leg and whining about Mr. Morthanos. "Bedtime," she said firmly.

When she and Todd left, I asked Dad about Mr. Morthanos's book. "Does he write poetry or stories or what?"

Dad looked up from the pipe he was lighting. "I believe he's trying to get a volume of poetry together. It sounds as if he's been working on it for years."

Poetry—how perfect. It was just what I imagined Mr. Morthanos writing. Unlike Dad, he wouldn't depend on a word processor or even a typewriter. He'd use a fountain pen with a fine, gold point. Sepia ink on ivory parchment, the kind calligraphers buy. His handwriting would swirl gracefully across the page.

When Susan came downstairs, she suggested inviting Mr. Morthanos to join us for a glass of wine by the fire. "If he's going to be here a long time, we might as well get acquainted."

While Dad puttered with the refreshments, Susan asked if I'd mind running up to Mr. Morthanos's room. "He's chosen the one at the end of the hall. I'd go myself but I'm just too tired to climb the steps more than once tonight."

I left the kitchen eagerly but halfway up the stairs my courage failed. Suppose Mr. Morthanos refused the invitation? Maybe he'd come here to be alone. He might not want to socialize.

In the hall below, I heard the tinkle of glasses. Dad was carrying a tray to the living room. Before he could look up and see me, I tiptoed to Mr. Morthanos's door, took a deep breath, and forced myself to knock, half-hoping he wouldn't hear me.

Mr. Morthanos opened the door as if he'd been expecting me. Behind him, a single candle burned on the desk, its quivering flame reflected in the window pane. In a pool of light, I saw a sheet of paper and a pen—the very scene I'd imagined, aglow in the shadows like an old painting.

"I'm sorry to disturb you, Mr. Morthanos, but we thought you might like to come down for a glass of wine by the fire." My voice came out as high and squeaky as a child's, and I blushed with embarrassment.

"You needn't be so formal, Cynda. Please call me Vincent." He smiled, freeing me to take a small breath. "Tell your parents I'll be happy to join them. I hope to become one of the family during my stay."

He lingered in the doorway, watching me with an intensity that made me uncomfortable. I wanted to leave, I wanted to stay, I wanted to be ten years older, pretty and sure of myself and as worldly as he.

Vincent smiled again. "Thank you for the invitation, Cynda."

I backed away uncertainly and tripped on the untied lace of my shoe. Humiliated, I turned and fled. What must Vincent Morthanos think of me? Why was I so shy, so clumsy? Why hadn't I at least tied my shoe before I'd gone upstairs?

7

By the time Vincent joined us, I'd managed to calm down, but I was still embarrassed about tripping on my shoelace. From across the room, I watched him make himself comfortable in an old armchair. His black sweater and jeans merged with the shadows, but his delicately boned face seemed to float against the darkness like a study in chiaroscuro.

While the adults sipped their wine and talked, I tried to read, but Vincent's presence distracted me. I was conscious of the creak of his chair, the rustle of his clothing, the sound of his voice. A remark about the environment, a comment on the political situation in Europe, a question concerning Dad's writing—every word Vincent spoke fascinated me, but I didn't have the courage to do more than listen. What could I say that he'd find interesting?

My opportunity finally came when Vincent asked Dad about the inn. "Such a delightful old place must have an interesting history," he said.

Dad smiled apologetically. "Susan and I have been here five years now, but all we know is that Underhill was built in the eighteenth century. It was a popular stopping place for travelers heading north."

"We've heard rumors it was once a smugglers' hideout," Susan put in. "I've been meaning to do some research on that, but it's hard to find the time."

"Surely a ghost or two haunts Underhill." Vincent's voice was light, almost mocking, but I sensed a deep interest underlying his words.

Dad and Susan both shook their heads, but I surprised myself by speaking up. "The cleaning woman, Mrs. Bigelow, says a girl who used to live here was murdered. She thinks her ghost haunts the inn."

I'd meant to impress Vincent, but Dad was the first to react. "No one ever told me anything about a murder," he said, frowning as if he doubted my word.

Ignoring Dad, Susan leaned toward me, worried and tense. "A girl was killed at Underhill, Cynda?"

I glanced at Vincent. He seemed as eager as Susan to hear what I had to say. "She wasn't killed in the inn itself," I began, "but outside, probably on the cliffs."

Without giving Dad a chance to interrupt, I repeated the details quickly. "Her killer was never caught, never punished," I concluded. "That's why she haunts the inn. She can't rest in peace till her death is avenged—and it never will be because the man who murdered her is dead himself now."

I glanced at Vincent. He was leaning back in his chair, lost in shadows. Only his hands caught the light, graceful and long-fingered. "Very interesting," he murmured.

Susan shuddered. "What an awful story, Cynda. Are you sure it's true?"

"True or not," Dad mused, "it gives me an idea for my next novel. Inspector Marathon could take a vacation in an historic inn. He'd hear about an old murder and use modern techniques to solve the crime. No ghosts, of course, nothing supernatural."

"Didn't Josephine Tey do something like that in one of her mysteries?" Susan asked. "If I remember correctly, a detective tries to prove Richard III couldn't have killed the little princes in the tower."

Vincent smiled at Susan. "You're thinking of *The Daughter of Time*, one of my personal favorites. Write a mystery half as good, Jeff, and your reputation will be made."

Dad beamed but Susan looked doubtful. "I've also read an Inspector Morse novel with a similar plot," she said.

"There are only so many plots to work with," Dad said. "Writers recycle them endlessly."

Before Dad could get started on this new subject, Vincent led the conversation back to the murdered girl. "Has anyone actually seen her ghost?"

"The only evidence we have is Mrs. Bigelow's uncanny feeling that something watches her when she's all alone," Dad said, making a joke of the old woman's fears.

Vincent turned to me. "Do you believe Mrs. Bigelow, Cynda?"

I hesitated. Vincent seemed genuinely interested, but I dreaded making a fool of myself in front of him.

Without looking at anyone, I said, "When Mrs. Bigelow was telling me about the girl, I felt a sort of sad, listening silence, just as if someone was in the room with us, someone we couldn't see. . . ."

I stumbled to a stop, too embarrassed to go on. It was hard to put these vague feelings into words with Dad staring at me as if I'd lost my mind.

"Mrs. Bigelow must be a better storyteller than I realized," he said. "She certainly put a spell on you with her talk of murder and restless spirits."

His teasing voice silenced me. Vowing to say no more, I watched the fire dance and leap on the hearth.

"You don't believe in ghosts, Jeff," Vincent said quietly.

"Absolutely not. When you die, you die, and that's that."

"You sound very certain." Vincent sat back in his chair, giving no clue to his feelings, but I was sure my father's attitude annoyed him as much as it did me.

"I *am* certain." Dad didn't bother to disguise the irritation creeping into his voice. "Surely you're too intelligent to put any credence in the tales of an ignorant old woman."

"On the contrary, Jeff, I agree with Hamlet." Vincent leaned forward and gazed into Dad's eyes. "'There are more things in heaven and earth, Horatio,'" he quoted, "'Than are dreamt of in your philosophy.'"

Vincent spoke with a quiet conviction that made me shiver, but Dad merely shrugged and said something about Shakespeare's gift for turning a phrase. I noticed that Susan didn't join in Dad's laughter. Like me, she huddled deeper into the sofa and folded her arms across her chest to ward off the cold.

I found my voice with difficulty. "Are you saying you believe in ghosts, Vincent?"

"Yes, Cynda, I most definitely do." As he spoke, a log fell in the fireplace and sent a shower of sparks racing up the chimney.

The noise startled us all, including Ebony. Uncoiling from his place beside me, he jumped off the couch and stalked toward the door. Halfway across the room, he noticed our guest and came to a dead stop. Vincent stretched a slender hand toward him, but Ebony sidestepped deftly and disappeared into the dark hall.

Seemingly indifferent to the cat's snub, Vincent rose to his feet. "I must bid you good night," he said. "If I encounter a ghost, I'll let you know tomorrow. In the meantime, sleep well."

The three of us watched our guest climb the stairs, his step almost as noiseless as Ebony's. After his door shut softly, Susan turned to Dad. "What a charming man," she said. "Handsome—and so mysterious."

Dad slid his arm around her waist. "Are you trying to make me jealous, Susie?"

She laughed. "Of course not, silly."

Dad turned to me. "Has Vincent won your heart too, Cynda?"

"He's very intelligent," I said, struggling to hide

my interest in our guest. "He knows so much about everything—history, politics . . ."

Dad agreed. "I wish we had more guests who enjoyed talking about something besides the weather."

"He's open-minded, too," I put in. "He didn't think what I said about ghosts was dumb."

That made Dad chuckle. Giving me a hug, he said, "I'm sorry, Cynda, but I can't help being a skeptic."

Susan looked sympathetic. "Face it, Cynda. Your father's a dreadful old cynic." Taking Dad's hand, she led him toward the stairs. "Let's call it a night, Jeff. Ghosts or no ghosts, I'm exhausted."

Dad paused to bank the fire. Then, giving me a quick kiss, he followed Susan. Without them, the room seemed cold and unnaturally still. I blew out the candles hastily and ran down the hall, resisting the urge to look behind me.

Safe in bed with Ebony curled up beside me, I lay awake a long time trying to sort out my feelings. As much as Vincent fascinated me, he made me uneasy. More than once I'd caught him looking at me with an intensity I didn't understand. His eyes were dark, unreadable—did he find me attractive or simply amusing? It was hard to imagine a man his age being interested in me, yet I could have sworn something intangible quivered in the air between us, a knowledge, a familiarity, a scary sense of destiny fulfilled.

When I fell asleep at last, Vincent followed me into my dreams. We were walking through the inn, but it had become a labyrinth of narrow halls and twisting corridors; I was lost, I wanted to get out, but every door I opened led to another room, darker and smaller than the one before. Vincent silenced my fears with laughter and kisses and promises. "You belong in the dark with me," he murmured. "I am the king of night and you are my queen."

*

I woke with his words ringing in my ears. Sunshine poured through the windows, filling the room with a dazzling white light. I smelled coffee brewing and muffins baking. In the hall, the clock struck nine.

Shivering in the cold air, I dressed carefully, taking more time than usual with my hair. I picked out my best black sweater, a soft angora turtleneck, and pulled on the jeans that fit best, a black pair like Vincent's.

Before I left my room I examined my face in the mirror. There was a tiny pimple in the corner of my mouth. If I picked it, it might get bigger. Or bleed. Better leave it alone and hope Vincent wouldn't notice.

I stopped for a moment outside the kitchen door and forced myself to breathe normally. Smoothing my hair, I stepped into the room, expecting to see Vincent at the table, but neither he nor Dad was there.

"Your father's already at work on his novel," Susan said, answering my unspoken questions. "Vincent doesn't eat breakfast. Tea in his room is all he wants. As for lunch, he asked me to leave a tray at his door so he can work all day undisturbed. We won't see him till dinner, I guess."

Without noticing my disappointment, Susan opened the morning paper and began working the daily crossword.

Todd looked up from his oatmeal. "Did you see Mr. Morthanos's car, Cynda?"

Susan drew the curtain aside. "Take a look, Cynda. It's a real beauty."

A car the color of moonlight on ice gleamed in the morning sunshine. A Porsche, Susan was saying, very powerful, very expensive—she hadn't realized there was so much money in poetry. Vincent must do something else, either that or he was independently wealthy. . . .

Scarcely listening, I stared at the Porsche. It was the car I'd seen passing the inn the night of the blizzard. I'd known it would return, and it had. I remembered the eerie flash of its headlights. Was it possible Vincent had heard my whispered invitation? Was that why he'd looked at me so intensely? The very thought sent a little shiver racing up and down my spine.

"I hate that car," Todd said loudly. "I hate Mr. Morthanos, too."

Susan touched his curls lightly. "Now, Todd, what did I tell you? Mr. Morthanos is our guest. You mustn't talk like that."

Ignoring his mother's rebuke, Todd asked, "Is Will coming to see us today?"

"This is Monday," Susan said. "Will's in school."

Todd sighed. "Maybe he'll come Saturday. We'll build another snowman, even bigger than the first one. We'll make new snow angels, too. The wind blew the others away, they flew up into the sky." He tugged my sleeve to get my attention. "Wasn't that the funnest day, Cynda, the day Will was here?"

For a second, I didn't know what Todd meant. I'd been thinking about Vincent, not listening to my brother. The day we'd played in the snow with Will seemed as long ago as childhood.

Todd studied my face. "You like Will, don't you, Cynda?"

"Of course," I said quickly. "He's very nice. You're lucky to have him for a friend." As I spoke, Will slipped further and further into the past. Compared to Vincent, he seemed no older than Todd, a friend from long ago, a boy as ordinary as a glass of milk.

"Will's your friend too," Todd said, frowning. "Or do you like Mr. Morthanos better now?"

Susan came to my rescue. "Todd, for heaven's sake, stop pestering your sister and eat your oatmeal. You hate it when it's cold."

*

Later, when I was alone in my room, I found it impossible to study. My algebra equations might as well have been bird tracks on snow, French verbs slipped from my memory, Greek and Roman dates jumbled hopelessly. The clock measured the minutes one by one, slowly ticking time away. So long till dinner, so long till I'd see Vincent.

62

The ceiling creaked. Someone on the second floor was walking slowly back and forth, back and forth. I closed my eyes and pictured the inn's layout. Vincent's room was at the end of the hall, right above mine. Those were his footsteps I heard, soft and deliberate, crisscrossing the floor overhead.

I sat still and listened, entranced by Vincent's nearness. The clock ticked, the wind blew, shadows shifted on the wall. Our guest continued to pace.

By noon I'd accomplished very little. Unless you counted the hundreds of times I'd written Vincent's name in my notebook.

8

When Vincent came downstairs at six o'clock, I was waiting for him in the hall. Dad, Susan, and Todd were already in the dining room, but I thought someone should greet Vincent. After all, this was his first dinner with us, a special occasion.

"Am I late, Cynda?"

Vincent's deep, curiously accented voice drove every clever word I'd planned to say right out of my head. "I wanted to show you where we eat, I was afraid you might not know, I . . ."

As I came to a stammering halt, Vincent thanked me for my consideration. "You look very nice," he added. "Black becomes you."

I looked down at my sweater as if I'd never seen it before. "My mother says black's not my color, it washes me out, makes me pale. She thinks I should wear blue or green, maybe even purple. . . ." I stopped, hot with confusion. Surely Vincent didn't care what my mother thought.

"Come," he said, touching my arm lightly. "We mustn't keep your family waiting."

We took seats opposite each other at the shiny

mahogany table. The setting was formal, the candle-light soft, the food cooked and presented perfectly by my father, both chef and waiter tonight. In the background, Wagner's "Siegfried-Idyll" played softly on the stereo. A fire crackled on the hearth.

The only problem was Todd. He sat beside me glumly, poking at his food and kicking the table leg in defiance of Susan's repeated pleas to sit still. Ignoring the handkerchief Dad handed him, he snuffled and sniffled and wiped his nose on his sleeve. He refused to look at Vincent or to answer any questions.

Todd wasn't cute tonight, nor was he funny. I shifted my chair away from him, ashamed of the way he was acting.

Vincent was obviously disturbed by Todd's behavior. Silent and withdrawn, he contributed little to the conversation Susan and Dad struggled to keep going. Like my brother, he spent more time rearranging his food than eating it. I caught his eye occasionally and tried to show my sympathy, but I couldn't rouse him from his thoughts.

When Todd knocked over an almost full glass of milk, Dad jumped up, thoroughly exasperated.

"That's enough, Todd."

Taking his son's arm, he pulled him none too gently away from the table.

Todd's tears upset Susan. Rescuing him from Dad, she said, "For God's sake, Jeff, have a little patience. He's been running a low-grade fever all day."

"Put him to bed then," Dad said. "If he's sick, that's where he belongs."

It was the first time I'd heard them quarrel.

"All right," Susan said, "I will." Taking Todd's hand, she led him upstairs. Long after they'd disappeared, we heard Todd crying.

Dad began to apologize, but Vincent stretched out his hand to stop him. "Please, Jeff," he said softly. "It is I who should apologize. For some reason my presence disturbs the child. Perhaps it would be better if I took all my meals in my room."

"Oh, no, Vincent," I said, and then felt my face flush.

Ignoring my emotional outburst, Vincent told Dad he'd join him later for a fireside chat. "But now, if you'll be kind enough to excuse me, I think I'll go upstairs."

After Vincent left, I gazed sadly at his abandoned plate. The salmon Dad had grilled so carefully was practically untouched, the baby carrots and wild rice barely disturbed.

I'd looked forward to dinner all day long, but in just a few minutes Todd had ruined everything. Sniffling and snuffling, kicking, pouting, spilling milk—why hadn't Dad taught him some manners? He let Todd get away with the most outrageous behavior just because he was little and cute. It wasn't fair. Todd should have been fed in the kitchen and put to bed before we sat down at the table.

*

True to his promise, Vincent came downstairs an hour or so later. Sinking into the same chair he'd chosen the night before, he accepted a glass of red wine and sipped it slowly.

Encouraged by a question from Vincent, Dad began talking about his novel. Despite five revisions, he was still bogged down in the second chapter.

"Every time I start a new book, I wonder if I'll be able to finish it," he admitted. "Beginnings are so damned hard. And then you get to the middle. After that, you have to face the end. Lord, sometimes I think I should have kept my teaching job."

Vincent twirled his glass slowly, nodding in agreement. "Writing's a long, slow process. It affords me so little pleasure I often wonder why I make the effort." One corner of his mouth rose sardonically. "Possibly because I can't do anything else."

Todd chose that moment to start screaming for Dad and Susan. "Come quick, there's a wolf under my bed," he yelled from the upstairs hall. "Oh, for God's sake, not another bad dream," Dad muttered, earning an angry look from Susan, who was already hurrying toward the stairs.

Dad got to his feet. "Excuse us, we'll be back in a few minutes." Glancing at me, he added, "Keep Vincent company, Cynda."

All day I'd dreamed of being alone with Vincent, but now that I was, my mouth was too dry to speak. I wanted to ask him about his car, I wanted to know where he'd been going in the snow, where he'd come from, but the silence grew, expanded, threatened to swallow me. I felt hot, then cold. I couldn't say a word.

Vincent looked at me inquiringly. "You seem uncomfortable, Cynda. Is something bothering you?"

Slowly, hesitantly, I said, "I saw your Porsche in the parking lot. It looks just like a car I saw the night it snowed. It slowed down at our driveway, flashed its lights, then drove on by . . ."

"So it was you I glimpsed at the window." Vincent leaned back in the chair and stretched his long legs toward the hearth. Firelight danced on the buckles of his boots. A ring on his right hand sparkled, a diamond stud in his ear glittered. "I sensed I'd be welcome here. That's why I returned. I hope I wasn't mistaken."

"Of course you're welcome," I said quickly. "Very welcome. I'm glad you're here. So's Dad. Susan too. We're all glad." I stopped, afraid of saying too much.

"Everyone but Todd," Vincent said wryly. "He certainly isn't enjoying my visit."

"I don't know what's wrong with him," I said. "It must be his cold or something. I hope he didn't hurt your feelings."

Vincent smiled. "Children are such funny little creatures, more like pets than human beings, as unpredictable as cats in their likes and dislikes."

I glanced at Ebony. He sat on the windowsill, as tall and aloof as an Egyptian cat statue I'd seen in the Metropolitan Museum of Art catalog. No friendlier than Todd, he refused to have anything to do with our guest.

Vincent raised his glass. The red wine glowed in

the firelight. "Just so you don't share your brother's feelings, Cynda."

"I don't share anything with Todd except my father," I said, eager to clarify things. "I'm staying here while my mother's in Italy with my stepfather."

"I thought as much," Vincent said slowly.

I stared at him, perplexed by the sympathy in his eyes. "What do you mean?"

Instead of answering, Vincent picked up one of the puzzles my father collected and left lying around for guests to solve. It looked deceptively easy. All you had to do was separate four cleverly linked circles. I'd tried to take them apart before dinner and given up ten or fifteen minutes later, totally frustrated.

Vincent's long, slender fingers shifted the circles, twisted and rearranged them. In a few seconds, he held one aloft. "Shall I tell your fortune, Cynda?"

I nodded, too fascinated to breathe, let alone speak.

"This circle is you," he said. Flourishing the other three, still joined, he added, "Jeff, Susan, and Todd."

Deftly he detached Dad's circle and joined it to mine. "How you'd like it to be." In a flash, he reunited Dad with Susan and Todd, leaving me unattached. "How it is."

Using circles instead of cards, Vincent had read my mind, unearthed my secrets. Speechless, I watched him remove another circle. He held up the two still joined. "Your mother and your stepfather."

We both stared silently at the circle lying on the table. My circle. Alone, unattached, easily forgotten.

69

Vincent swiftly reassembled the puzzle. The only sound was the clink of silver circles. When he'd finished, he crossed the room and sat on the couch beside me. "Believe me, Cynda, I understand. I know how hard it is to be an outsider, alone and unhappy, misunderstood." Resting his head against the back of the couch, he sighed and closed his eyes.

This close to him, I was conscious of his smooth skin, his dark hair, his long fingers. He smelled of spices, sweet and aromatic. His sweater was cashmere, as thick and soft and strokeable as Ebony's fur. He was beautiful, I thought, almost unearthly in his perfection. How could such a handsome man empathize so completely with my loneliness? Surely he had no end of friends and admirers.

Vincent opened his eyes and gazed at me. In the silence, the fire whispered to the logs, consuming them softly, lovingly. For a moment, I thought he meant to kiss me, but the strange intimacy he'd created was destroyed by the sound of voices. Susan and Dad were coming downstairs.

"I must go now, Cynda." Vincent got to his feet quickly. "We'll talk again."

I reached toward him, wishing he'd stay, but he didn't turn back. Passing Dad and Susan in the hallway, he bid them a polite good night. Then, head erect, he climbed the stairs and disappeared into the darkness at the top.

Dad and Susan looked at each other, puzzled perhaps by Vincent's abrupt departure.

"I guess the poor guy got tired of waiting for us to

come back," Dad said. "We had the devil of a time getting Todd to settle down and go to sleep."

Susan collapsed on the couch beside me. "I hope you and Vincent found something interesting to talk about while we were gone."

Without looking up from my book, I said, "He's very nice."

Susan squeezed my hand. "Yes," she agreed, "he *is* nice, but . . ."

I thought she'd say more about Vincent, but instead she asked if I'd mind fixing a pot of chamomile tea. Todd had worn her out, left her tense and worried. A cup of hot tea was just what she needed to relax.

While I waited for the kettle to boil, I gazed out the window. An almost full moon shone down on the snowman, casting his inky black shadow on the white lawn and hiding his face. The wind plucked at his scarf. The moon slid behind a cloud, darkening the scene. When it emerged, I had the oddest sensation that the snowman had moved closer to the inn, taking tiny steps like a child playing a game.

In the woods, the owl called three times. At the same moment, the wind rose, filling the air with a fine dust of blown snow that almost obscured the lonely figure. I turned away, afraid the snowman might be nearer when the wind dropped.

9

Several days passed, each like the one before. In the mornings I studied—or tried to—while Dad worked on his novel and Susan sewed. After lunch, it was back to the books for a couple of hours. In the late afternoon, I took care of Todd while Susan napped and Dad wrote. At six, we ate dinner. At seven, Todd went to bed. At eight, Vincent joined us for a glass of wine and an hour or so of conversation.

Every night I hoped Todd would wake from a bad dream and yell for Dad and Susan, but he slept soundly, depriving me of a chance to be alone with Vincent. I had to content myself with being in the same room with him. From my perch on the couch, I listened to every word he said and stole looks at him as often as I dared. Sometimes he caught me watching him; sometimes I caught him watching me.

Although I rarely had anything to say, Vincent made an effort to draw me into the conversation. Unlike Dad, he took my opinions seriously. He listened to me. He never laughed or teased me. If I made a mistake, he defended me, even when my error was as irrefutable as a misquoted poem or a blunder in grammar. He had a clever way of making Dad sound like a pedant when he corrected me.

Vincent also noticed how often Susan asked me to do things for her. Fetch this, fetch that, make tea, clean up the dishes, put another log on the fire, let the cat in, let the cat out, answer the phone. When I returned from one of these chores, he'd catch my eye and smile sympathetically.

*

One afternoon I took a walk to escape Todd's endless requests to build block towers, play Candyland, help him with puzzles, read to him, and so on. Sometimes I enjoyed entertaining my brother, but he was so demanding. One game was never enough, neither was one book or one puzzle. More, more, more—it was exhausting.

From the top of the cliff, I looked down uneasily, half expecting to see the dead girl's body awash in the surf. But the ocean was empty. Waves rolled toward shore, their sleek, green backs streaked with seaweed. A gust of wind ran its cold fingers through my hair and I turned away. It was a sad and lonely place, made more so by Mrs. Bigelow's story.

I walked cautiously down the path to the beach. Soothed by the rumble of the surf and the cries of gulls, I hiked along the shore for miles, enjoying the solitude and the freedom to think my own thoughts—mainly about Vincent.

By the time I turned back, the sun had set, leaving a gash of red in the western sky. On the horizon, the sea merged with the dark clouds. The foam on the breaking waves glowed pink in the dull light.

Just ahead, a barely discernible figure emerged from the mist. I was alone. Night was falling fast. The moon was already visible, small and shrouded, giving little light. The murdered girl came to mind again, and I was afraid. I shouldn't have walked so far, shouldn't have stopped so often to pick up shells and stones, should have remembered how short winter days are and how soon it gets dark.

"Cynda, is that you?"

"Vincent!" Weak-kneed with relief, I hurried toward him.

"What are you doing out here all by yourself?" he asked. "It's almost dark, you should be home. Susan is looking for you."

"She probably wants me to set the table," I grumbled, "or keep Todd out of her hair."

Vincent agreed. "She demands a great deal from you."

I looked at him gratefully. Most adults would have taken up for Susan. "She's pregnant," they would have said. "She has a right to expect help." But Vincent saw things from my point of view. Susan was taking advantage of me.

We walked along in silence. The waves washed in and out, sucking at the sand. In the distance, well back from the cliffs, I could just make out the inn's candles.

"Do you ever wonder where the murdered girl's body was found?" Vincent asked suddenly.

I shivered and said nothing. The girl had been on my mind all afternoon. I didn't want to think about her anymore. What I wanted now was romance. Maybe even a kiss. . . .

I glanced at Vincent hopefully, but he was gazing at the cliff tops and the sky beyond. Stars twinkled here and there, appearing one by one in rifts between the ragged clouds. "Some people believe evil lingers at the scene of a crime for years afterward," he said slowly. "Perhaps forever."

"Don't say any more, Vincent," I whispered. "Please don't."

"I'm sorry," he said, coming closer. "I didn't mean to frighten you, Cynda."

Vincent took my hand and we walked on. "As you come to know me better," he said, "you'll discover I have a morbid streak which may not be to your liking."

I stared up at him, thrilled by his nearness and the touch of his hand. "I can't imagine disliking anything about you, Vincent."

His grip tightened. "You've just met me, Cynda. You have no idea what sort of man I am." He was smiling, teasing me, his voice full of humor.

"That's true," I said, trying to match his bantering tone. "I don't know where you were born, where you live, what sort of family you have. Why, I don't even know how old you are."

"I'm older than you think," Vincent said lightly.

"You can't be more than thirty."

He laughed. "Give or take a few centuries."

I laughed too, sharing the joke, and he gave my hand a squeeze.

We'd come to the path leading to the cliff top. Vincent stopped walking and studied my face in the dim light. "Much as I enjoy your company, I suggest you go home before someone comes looking for you. I wouldn't want your father to get the wrong idea about me."

Something dark and rich in his voice made my face burn, not with embarrassment but with pleasure. "Let's walk a little farther," I said. "I don't want to go back to the inn yet."

"Believe me, I'd like to keep you with me." Vincent spoke so softly I barely heard him as he slowly backed away.

"Where are you going?" I reached out to stop him but he was already several feet distant, merging with the dark sea and sky.

"I'll walk for a while," he said, "and think of you, Cynda." With that, he vanished into the sea mist.

I took a few hesitant steps after him but the wind was rising fast. Sand stung my face and eyes, and I turned onto the path, reluctant to let him go but warmed by his words.

*

When I opened the kitchen door several minutes later, Susan was waiting for me. "Where have you been, Cynda?"

"I went for a walk on the beach," I said, avoiding

her eyes. If she were anything like Mom, she'd guess I was hiding something.

"You were gone for more than an hour," Susan said. "I was worried."

She seemed willing to let the subject drop, so I apologized, but I couldn't help being annoyed. I didn't need Susan to play the part of my mother. She wasn't old enough to tell me what to do or what not to do.

Vincent returned while Todd and I were playing Candyland, but he slipped upstairs without saying more than hello.

Todd made a face at Vincent's back. "Did you see him when you were walking on the beach?"

I moved my playing piece slowly and deliberately along the game's curving path. "No," I lied. "I didn't see Vincent."

A few minutes later, Susan called me to the kitchen. "Can you take Vincent's tray to him? I've just started another batch of hollandaise sauce. It will curdle if I leave it."

Unable to believe my good luck, I picked up the tray and climbed the stairs. The door opened before I'd even raised my hand to knock. "Come in," Vincent said, "come in."

As I passed him, my shoulder brushed his arm. I tried to hold the tray steady, but the carafe tipped, spilling red wine on the white napkin, like drops of blood on snow.

"Let me have that." Vincent's fingers touched mine as he took the tray. He carried it to a small table near the fire and set it down carefully beside a stack of paper, a pen, a bottle of ink, and a pile of books, testimony to his day's work.

He lifted the lid covering his dinner plate and pierced the steak with his fork. When the juices ran out, he smiled. "Extra rare, just as I requested. Please give my compliments to the chef."

Nervously I shifted my weight from one foot to the other, not sure if I should stay or leave. "Do you want anything else?" I asked, thinking he might like more pepper, a sauce, something I could fetch for him.

Vincent raised his head and gazed at me. His eyes lingered on my lips and then moved to my breasts. He said nothing. He didn't need to.

The air thickened with the smell of burning logs and melting candle wax, of steak and cloves. The only sounds were the crackle of the fire and the murmur of the wind. My heart pounded, jackhammering against my ribs like a wild thing.

Vincent smiled as if he heard every beat of my heart, but when I took a step closer, he shook his head. "You mustn't keep your family waiting."

*

Vincent came down later for his glass of wine, and he and Dad got into a discussion of politics, a subject I knew little about. While they talked, Susan sewed and I leafed through an anthology of poetry. From time to time, I glanced at Vincent. More than once I caught him staring at me, his eyes dark with promises that made my heart beat faster.

The conversation went on and on, as relentless as the wind buffeting the inn. Occasionally Susan made a remark, but no one asked for my opinion. My eyelids grew heavy, and my head nodded; the words on the page jumbled, made no sense. When I woke up, the fire had burned low, Dad and Susan were asleep, and Vincent was sitting beside me, smiling as if my confusion amused him.

"I'm afraid my discourse on European economic problems put everyone to sleep," he said apologetically.

Taking my poetry book, he turned the pages slowly as if he were looking for something. The paper rustled like silk. "'The Highwayman,'" he said, stopping at last. Without taking his eyes from mine, he began to recite:

> The wind was a torrent of darkness among the
>   gusty trees,
> The moon was a ghostly galleon tossed upon
>   cloudy seas,
> The road was a ribbon of moonlight over the
>   purple moor,
> And the highwayman came riding—
> Riding— riding—
> The highwayman came riding, up to the old
>   inn-door.

Vincent paused. "How familiar it sounds. An old inn on a cold moonlit night, a lover seeking 'the landlord's black-eyed daughter, Bess, the landlord's daughter, Plaiting a dark red love-knot into her long black hair.'"

Closing the book soundlessly, he threw his head back and sighed. "What a girl Bess was. Can you imagine loving a man enough to die for him?"

"Yes," I whispered, staring at his face. "I'd do anything for the person I loved."

"It's one thing to sit by the fire and speak of dying for love," Vincent said, "but to do it, actually to die— No, Cynda, I don't think many girls would. Not willingly."

He reached out to caress my cheek. His fingers were cool, his touch light, but his eyes were dark. "So pretty," he whispered, "so sweet, so trusting—what a dear girl you are, Cynda. I fear I could fall in love with you."

Leaning closer, he brushed my lips with his. Before I had a chance to speak or move, he got to his feet and crossed the room as silently as Ebony. He'd no sooner settled himself in his chair than Dad and Susan woke up and smiled sheepishly at each other.

Susan looked at the clock. "Goodness, it's not quite ten. I don't know why I'm so sleepy."

"You've had a long day," Vincent said sympathetically. "While Jeff and I indulge ourselves with our writing, you cook and care for everyone. I don't know how you do so much—and do it so magnificently."

Obviously flattered, Susan shrugged and said it was nothing, anyone could do what she did, but Vincent insisted she was a marvel. He praised the inn's decor, the beautiful objects in the living room, her sewing projects. I would have been jealous had he not smiled at me occasionally as if we shared a joke at Susan's expense.

When Vincent finally ran out of compliments, Dad suggested a game of Scrabble. We cleared a space on a small table near the fire and crowded around the board. I was so close to Vincent our knees touched, our shoulders bumped, our fingers brushed against each other's. It was impossible for me to concentrate on the game. After two rounds, I was clearly losing, but I didn't care. Being near Vincent was all I wanted.

When the clock struck eleven, Susan yawned and stretched. "I don't know about the rest of you, but I'm too tired to spell my own name."

She rose to leave but Dad stopped her. "Look, Susie. We've made a sentence." Pointing at the words zigzagging across the board, he read aloud, "Ill come to thee by moonlight."

Except for "moonlight," the words were parts of other, longer words—a syllable here, a letter there, snaking from one square to another; up, down, and across, a secret message for us to find.

"Ill come to thee." Susan crossed her arms protectively and shuddered. "It sounds like a curse."

I stared at the board, "The Highwayman" fresh in my mind. "It should be *I'll*, not *ill*," I whispered. "Don't you see? There's no apostrophe in Scrabble. It says 'I'll come to thee by moonlight.'"

I stole a glance at Vincent, and he nodded approvingly.

"Yes, of course," Dad said. "'The Highwayman'—

'Look for me by moonlight, Watch for me by moonlight, *I'll* come to thee by moonlight.'"

Susan looked at me. "How did you do it, Cynda?"

"I didn't," I said. "I'm not that clever."

Dad turned to Vincent. "It must be your handiwork, Vince."

Vincent smiled mysteriously. "Maybe, maybe not."

Dad stroked his beard and frowned. "Surely you're not saying this happened by chance."

"Of course not. Nothing happens by chance." Vincent seemed to find our bewilderment humorous. "Perhaps it's a message from your resident ghost."

Susan shivered and drew closer to Dad. Putting his arm around her, he said, "When I'm not so sleepy, you can tell me how you did it, Vince."

Vincent followed them upstairs, chuckling at something Dad said. In the light of the dying fire, I studied the message on the Scrabble board. With trembling fingers, I picked up the wooden tiles and dropped them one by one into the box. "Ill" or "I'll"—a curse or a promise?

10

An hour or so later, Vincent stepped out of the shadows and into the moonlight. I'd been waiting at the window, watching and listening, certain he'd meant the message on the Scrabble board for me. I'd heard his footsteps on the floor above me, I'd heard him tiptoe down the stairs, I'd heard the back door open and close softly. Now he walked toward me, tall and lean in his long, dark coat, as graceful as a line of poetry slanting across the blank snow.

Ebony crouched beside me. The moment I opened the window, he leaped out and vanished like a black arrow shot into the night.

"Come back," I called softly, fearing he'd freeze.

"Let him go," Vincent said. "Hunters must have their sport as well as their comfort."

He smiled and rested his hands on the windowsill. His fingers were long and thin, his nails neatly clipped, well cared for. Beside his, my hands were clumsy, my nails chewed and uneven.

"I've come to you by moonlight, Cynda."

"Yes," I whispered. "I've looked for you, watched for you."

We gazed at each other silently. From the woods, the owl called. Once, twice, three times. The spooky sound made me shudder but Vincent turned his head and listened as if the owl spoke to him and him alone.

When the last echo faded into the dark, he sighed, his breath a silver plume in the cold air. "Come for a walk with me, Cynda. It's too lovely a night to stay indoors."

Quickly, fearing he'd change his mind if I dawdled, I pulled on my parka and gloves and wrapped a scarf around my neck. He offered his hand and helped me climb through the window. I'd heard girls brag about sneaking outside to be with their boyfriends, but I'd never dreamed of doing it myself.

I looked back once. Except for the candles, the inn's windows were dark. Yet I was sure someone was watching, sure someone saw Vincent take my hand and hurry me away.

"What's the matter?" Vincent slid his arm around my waist to shield me from the wind. "Is the night too cold for you?"

"I think someone saw us."

Vincent turned and studied the inn. "Everyone's asleep."

"How can you tell?"

"Common sense. If they were awake, we'd see lights. Movement."

Hand in hand, we walked toward the ocean. I tried to match my step with his, but, even though our legs were about the same length, his stride was longer. He seemed to glide across the snow effortlessly.

When we reached the cliff top, Vincent turned to me. The wind whipped his hair back, exposing his high forehead. His long coat billowed like a cape. "Are you frightened to be out here alone with me on a wild winter night?"

I encircled his neck with my arms, amazed by my daring. "I'd go anywhere with you," I whispered, "and never be afraid."

He smiled and drew me closer. I felt the strong beat of his heart, then his mouth against mine. Not just a brush of his lips, but a real kiss, a kiss so wonderful I wanted it to last till the stars burned out, till the ocean shrank to a drop, till time circled back on itself and began all over again.

"We must go," Vincent murmured at last. "It's late, and the wind is blowing harder."

I clung to him, so weak with love I feared I'd fall if he let me go. "No, not yet," I begged. "It's so beautiful I want to stay here forever."

"We'll come back again, Cynda, I promise. Every night if you wish."

Vincent kissed me once more and led me away from the cliff, away from the black sea laced with foam, away from the moon sailing from cloud to cloud like a ghostly galleon. I trudged beside him, pushed homeward by the wind, stumbling in the deep snow, wanting nothing but his kisses. Like Juliet, I prayed the gentle night would last forever, loving, black-browed night. Never again would I pay worship to the garish sun.

After he helped me climb through my window,

Vincent lingered outside, holding my hands in his. "Promise to keep our meetings secret," he whispered. "If your father or Susan knew, they'd send me away."

"I'll never tell," I swore. "I'd rather die than lose you, Vincent."

"My sweet darling." He kissed me tenderly, raised his hand in farewell, and vanished into the night like a spiral of smoke blown by the wind.

Long after he was gone, I stood at the open window, gazing into the darkness, yearning for him to return. Another kiss, a few more minutes of his time. Finally the cold drove me to bed. Huddled under the covers, I fell asleep with Vincent's name on my lips.

*

The next afternoon, Susan rapped on my door to tell me Will was in the kitchen. "He's on his way to Ferrington to pick up some groceries. I know you're studying, but I need cereal and milk. Could you ride along with him?"

I wasn't in the mood to see Will, but she insisted. "I'd go myself, but I'm up to here with sewing projects."

Reluctantly I followed her to the kitchen. Todd and Will sat next to each other at the table. "Draw Captain Jupiter on his horse," Todd begged. "Make him fight another wolf."

Will saw me and smiled. "Later, Todd. Cynda and I have errands to run."

"Can I come too?"

Susan took Todd's hand. "Not this time."

Todd let out a bellow of complaint, but Susan hushed him with promises of hot chocolate and a story.

Pulling on my parka, I followed Will outside. His old truck was parked beside Vincent's Porsche.

"What a fantastic car." Will walked around the Porsche slowly, running a hand over its sleek body, admiring its lines. "Grandmother said Mr. Morthanos drove something fancy."

I peered through the car's windshield at the cozy interior and pictured myself riding into Ferrington with Vincent. We'd glide through the snowy countryside, swaying around curves, listening to soft music, sitting so close our hands and legs might touch. Dark and cold outside, dark and warm inside. Cradled close in soft leather seats as red as blood. . . . Vincent and me, Vincent.

Before I climbed into Will's truck, I looked up at Vincent's window. He was staring down at me, his face as pale as the moon's in a winter sky. When he saw me, he smiled and drew the drapes.

"So that's Mr. Morthanos," Will said. "Grandmother's been here twice since he came, but she hasn't seen him yet. She says he doesn't want to be disturbed, not even to have his room cleaned."

"Vincent's a poet," I said, treasuring the sound of his first name. "He writes all day. If he's interrupted, he loses his inspiration."

Will snorted. "He sounds like a real prima donna."

"How can you say that?" I glared at Will. "I've

never known anyone as nice as Vincent. He's quiet and sensitive and very intelligent."

"Todd doesn't think much of him," Will said. "The minute I walked in the door he started talking about how awful he is."

"You can't judge anyone by what Todd says. Dad told me he either likes people or hates them—for no reason at all."

Will grinned. "That's true. A man stayed at the inn last summer, one of a bunch of German tourists. Every time poor Herr Schroeder tried to be friendly, Todd was rude to him. Your father was embarrassed, but Herr Schroeder was very understanding."

Knowing how much Will liked Todd, I decided to keep my thoughts about my brother to myself. Will wouldn't agree that Todd was spoiled; he'd take up for him just as everyone else did.

Will forgot about Vincent when we passed a pair of deer watching us from the woods. "Aren't they beautiful? I'd love to draw them but they'd be gone before I could find a pencil."

He drove on slowly, pointing out things here and there—a place where blueberries grew, a curve in the river where he'd caught a big trout, an old barn he'd drawn.

By the time we got to Ferrington, I was laughing at Will's stories about Rockpoint High. It seemed the kids gave the teachers a hard time; they were always cutting up and saying funny things. Will was good at imitating their Down-East accents, but I had a feeling Susan was right about his not having many friends. It sounded as if he spent most of his school day watching and listening.

In sunlight, the town looked even worse than it had the night Dad and I stopped at the diner. Smaller, shabbier. Stores closed, boarded up, posted with fliers advertising last summer's events. Sea gulls floated overhead, complaining to one another. A cat slunk past, followed by an empty plastic bag drifting across the ice like a tired ghost.

Will pointed down a narrow street to the harbor. "In the summer, all kinds of places open up by the water—T-shirt shops, coffeehouses, ice cream stands, souvenir stores. Everything your heart desires at twice the price you'd pay back home."

It was hard to imagine summer. Impossible. Huge mounds of snow encased houses and buried shrubbery. Icicles as thick as my arm hung like stalactites from roofs. Sheets and towels were frozen on clotheslines. Bare trees creaked in the cold wind. I thought of Mom in warm, sunny Italy and shivered enviously.

"How about a cup of coffee at the diner?" Will asked. "We can get the groceries afterwards."

Gina was at the cash register, ringing up a sale, but as soon as she was free she came to take our order. She seemed pleased to see me with Will.

"I hear you have a guest," she said. "A real odd duck."

"Mr. Morthanos is a poet," said Will, the master of sarcasm. "You know the type—very sensitive."

Gina eyed him as if she weren't sure of his meaning. "My Aunt Elsie was a poet. She wrote little verses for holidays and special occasions, even got some published in the local paper, but she didn't lock herself up in her room to do it. Aunt Elsie was as sweet and friendly as a person can be, perfectly normal in every way."

After Gina left, Will grinned at me, but I didn't smile back. "I wish you'd stop making fun of Vincent," I said. "He's a serious poet, Will, not a jingle writer like Gina's Aunt Elsie."

The booth squeaked as Will shifted his position. "I was just teasing you. Why do you care what I say about Vincent? He's just some old guy staying at the inn."

"He's not old."

Will sighed. "Okay, he's not old, he's not a prima donna. He's a great poet, Walt Whitman's equal. Quiet, sensitive, intelligent—is that what you said?"

"It's close enough." I turned my coffee cup round and round. It made a harsh sound as it scraped across the sugar I'd spilled on the table. What would Will say if I told him I was in love with Vincent? Even though I didn't know Will very well, I could guess. He'd tell me to stay away from Vincent, he'd say I was a fool to trust him.

What if Will was right? How did I know what Vincent really wanted from me? Maybe it had been a mistake to sneak out the window, maybe I shouldn't have let him kiss me. There was no telling what a kiss meant to a man his age. Or where it might lead.

Suddenly worried, I leaned across the table to get Will's attention. He looked up from the sea gull he

90

was doodling on his place mat. His face was closed, guarded. "We should go," he said. "The store closes at six."

The time to confide in Will had passed. He wasn't interested in anything now but buying the groceries and taking me back to the inn. I gulped down my coffee, grabbed my jacket, and followed him to the cash register.

"Come back soon," Gina said as we left. "Both of you."

Will didn't look at me, but his face reddened. I blushed too. We walked out of the diner without speaking. The space between us was just the right size for Vincent.

11

By the time we left Ferrington, I was glad I hadn't confided in Will. That flash of uncertainty in the diner had probably been the result of his sarcastic remarks. I shouldn't have let them bother me. I loved Vincent, I trusted him. How could I have considered betraying him?

At the inn, Will insisted on carrying the groceries inside. Susan invited him to stay for dinner. Todd was delighted, but I wasn't at all pleased. During the meal, I said little, hoping to discourage Will from lingering after we finished eating, but he didn't notice. Not with Todd sitting beside him, begging him to draw pictures and play games. Not with Susan offering him a second helping of cherry cobbler. Not with Dad asking him to stay and meet Vincent—the very thing I dreaded.

After Susan took an unwilling Todd to bed, Dad led Will into the living room. "Vincent's an interesting chap," he said. "I think you'll like him."

"I've heard a lot about him already." Will glanced at me, but I picked up my poetry book and pretended to read, determined not to let him get a rise out of me again.

When Vincent came downstairs, Dad introduced Will. Vincent shook his hand and smiled, but Will seemed embarrassed, unsure of himself. Compared to Vincent, he was awkward and clumsy, a boy in faded jeans and a bulky plaid shirt, his feet enormous in scuffed work boots, his curly hair untidy, his cheeks as red as a child's.

"Jeff showed me some of your artwork," Vincent said, making an effort to put Will at ease. "A ship at sea, a lighthouse, gulls, Todd's Captain Jupiter slaying a wolf. You're very talented."

Will mumbled his thanks and took a seat beside me. Vincent went on talking to Will, showing an interest in him that made me jealous. He asked about his formal training, where he intended to study, what he hoped to do with his ability.

Will stumbled through his answers, speaking in halting monosyllables. It was obvious he didn't enjoy Vincent's attention. Finally he got to his feet. "I told Grandmother I'd be home by ten. She doesn't like to be alone at night."

He edged toward the hall, but his eyes lingered on me. I had an idea he hoped I'd walk to the door with him.

Quick to pick up on things, Susan said, "Show Will where his jacket is, Cynda."

Reluctantly I led Will out of the cozy living room. The hall was cold and dark. Behind me, I heard Vincent laugh at something Dad said.

I pulled Will's bulky parka out of the crowded coat closet and handed it to him. He took it wordlessly and held it for a moment. "I don't like him," he said at last.

"How can you say that? Vincent was so interested in your art, he was so encouraging. He praised you, Will Bigelow."

Will shook his head. "He didn't mean a word he said, Cynda. He's a con man if I ever saw one."

"You're as bad as Todd."

"People say kids and dogs are good judges of character," Will said. "Why not include cats, too? I noticed Ebony left the room when Vincent came in."

"Don't be silly. Everybody knows cats are the most persnickety things on earth."

Will sighed and zipped his parka. "Maybe I'm just jealous," he said. Without looking at me again, he opened the kitchen door and vanished into the cold night.

For a moment I stood there staring at the door. Once I would have been thrilled to have a boyfriend as nice as Will Bigelow. But that was before I met Vincent.

When I returned to the living room, Vincent smiled at me over the rim of his glass. "What a pleasant young man Will is," he said. "So shy and unassuming, yet so talented and handsome."

I sank down on the couch without replying and picked up my book. Something told me Dad and Susan had concocted a romance between Will and me. While I'd been out of the room, they'd probably discussed the possibility with Vincent. Maybe that's what they'd been laughing at.

94

When Vincent got up to leave, I raised my head and caught his eye. He gave me a long, considering smile. "Good night, Cynda," he said softly.

I waited a few minutes, listening to him climb the stairs. When the inn was silent again, I closed my book, said good night to Susan, kissed Dad, and went to my room.

*

Vincent came to my window that night and the next. Night after night, he led me across the snow and into the dark. Although I wanted to learn more about him, he had a way of turning the conversation back to me. He drew every sorrow from my heart, every pain; he never wearied of hearing how deeply my parents' divorce had hurt me, how much I'd cried when Dad left, how jealous I was of Todd and Susan, how much I resented my stepfather.

The more I talked, the more he sympathized, and the angrier I became with my parents. First I stopped answering Mom's letters. Then I stopped reading them. I stuffed the envelopes into a drawer unopened. Why bother? They were all the same— pages and pages of flowery accounts of the fun she and Steve were having in Italy, a paragraph at the end asking about me, "Love You" scrawled at the bottom like an afterthought.

As for Susan and Dad, my resentments multiplied and our arguments grew. Like Mom, Susan found fault with everything I did or didn't do—why didn't I pick up after myself? Why was I so careless about turning lights off? You'd think leaving a coffee cup on the table signaled the end of civilization.

Dad spent more time than ever in his den, grumbling and complaining. Instead of feeling close to him I felt more and more distant. When I accused him of loving Todd more than me, he told me to grow up.

Vincent was the only one who understood, the only one who listened, the only one who cared how I felt. He comforted me with tender words and fierce kisses.

One night, his teeth grazed my skin, and I pulled away, startled by the pain. He held me tighter, murmuring apologies, seeking my neck with his lips gently, softly, sweetly, persuading me till I was willing to let him do what he wished—no matter what it was.

In the morning, I noticed a little red mark on my neck. A girl I once knew used to show me similar marks—love bites, she called them. Her boyfriend gave them to her, she said, giggling. Other girls called them hickeys. Even though they bragged about them, they hid them with scarves or turtlenecks.

I touched the mark curiously, thrilled by the way my skin tingled, and pulled up the collar of my sweater. If Susan saw it, she might suspect something was going on between Vincent and me. That wouldn't do. She mustn't find out.

*

That night, as Vincent and I crossed the lawn, he suddenly tensed and looked back at the inn. Except for the candles, its windows were dark, but on the third floor, a face was pressed against the glass.

Seizing my hand, he hurried me into the shadows.

"Was it Susan?" I whispered.

"No," he said. "Todd."

"What if he tells?"

"Deny it, say he was dreaming. Everyone knows the child is fearful and overly imaginative."

Somewhere in the woods, the owl called, and Vincent turned to listen. We'd reached the middle of the field that lay between the inn and the ocean. From where we stood, I could hear the surf.

The moon shone full on Vincent's face; its cold light gave his features a cruel, hawklike sharpness I'd never noticed. "The hunter is abroad," he said softly.

The owl called again, nearer this time. Vincent took me in his arms. Eager for his kiss, I lifted my face and closed my eyes.

Vincent drew in his breath. His lips moved from my mouth to my throat again. I felt a flash of pain sharper than before, as quick as the jab of a needle. The stars and moon spun and I spun with them, whirling faster and faster into darkness.

Suddenly the wind rose with a shriek. At the same moment, Vincent made a choking sound and thrust me away.

I staggered for a moment and almost fell. "What's wrong?" I cried, reaching out for him.

He kept his head turned, hiding his face. The wind seemed to push him away from me. He fought it, cursing as if it were an adversary. "Go back to the inn!" he shouted to make himself heard above the gale.

I reached again for his hand, but windblown snow, as fine and hard as diamond dust, blinded me. "Vincent, don't leave me!" I whirled in circles, searching for him. "Where are you?"

The wind's voice filled my ears, I heard nothing else. Dizzy with panic, I stumbled about calling Vincent's name. He couldn't have left me, couldn't have abandoned me. Yet I neither saw nor heard him. He seemed to have vanished into the cold, snowy darkness.

Without him to guide me, I was lost. I had no idea where the inn was, which direction to take. The wind and blowing snow confused me, left me too weak to walk. Despite the cold, I sank down in the snow and lay on my back, staring up at the black sky begemmed with stars. The moon sat among them, surrounded by a pale nimbus. Beautiful, I thought drowsily, so beautiful is the queen of night.

The wind dropped, its voice changed to a low moan. Cold fingers caressed my face and smoothed my hair. "Ill has come to you," the wind whispered, "to me, to all of us . . ."

A girl as pale as sea-foam stood over me, barely visible in the eddying snow. Without actually speaking, she urged me to stand, to walk. Like the wind at my back, she helped me along, she guided me toward the inn's candles, she hovered near me till she was sure I was safely in bed. Then she vanished, leaving behind the faintest trace of the sea.

I hovered on the edge of consciousness, trying to understand what had happened. But I was too tired to think, too cold. I closed my eyes and sank into a deep, dreamless sleep.

12

I spent the morning trying to sort out last night's jumble of memories and dreams. I remembered Todd's face at the window, Vincent's hard, hurtful kisses, a fierce wind blowing us apart. Then a pale girl bending over me, taking my hand, leading me to the inn.

The more I thought about it all, the more confused I felt. I couldn't sit still, couldn't concentrate. I had to see Vincent, had to talk to him. My questions couldn't wait till he came to my window hours from now.

He was just above, pacing the floor, apparently as restless as I. What if I sneaked upstairs to his room? Who'd see? Who'd know?

Cautiously I opened my door and listened. There was no sound from Dad's den, but I knew he was hard at work on his novel. From the third floor, I heard the whir of Susan's sewing machine. Todd was probably with her. They were all busy, they weren't thinking about me.

Quickly, silently, I ran up the steps to the second floor. Before I raised my hand to knock, Vincent opened the door and drew me inside.

"Thank God, you're safe," he whispered. "I searched everywhere for you, but the snow blinded me, the wind drove me away, I couldn't find you."

I clung to him, weeping. "She came for me, she led me home."

Vincent pulled back to stare at me. "What are you talking about? Who came for you?"

"The murdered girl," I whispered, trembling in spite of myself. "She brought me to the inn. If she hadn't, I would have died in the snow."

His hands tightened on my shoulders. "You must have been dreaming, Cynda."

"I saw her face, I heard her voice."

"A dream," Vincent repeated, "just a dream." His voice was deep and comforting. He kissed me gently, stroked my hair, held me close. The steady beat of his heart soothed me, his words convinced me. "Forget last night. You're safe now. That's all that matters."

I raised my face, hoping he'd kiss me again. On my lips or on my throat, I didn't care where. Just so he kissed me. Just so he loved me.

"Not now, Cynda." Vincent sighed and released me. "It's too dangerous."

I watched him sit down at his writing table. Even though it was the middle of the morning, his room was dark, the curtains tightly drawn. The only light came from the candle illuminating his books and papers.

"Let me stay a little longer," I begged. "I won't bother you. I promise."

Vincent picked up his pen. "Suppose Susan or Jeff should find you here?"

"They're busy, they don't care where I am or what I'm doing." I reached across the table for his hand, but in my haste, I knocked the candle over. Its flame ignited a heap of papers. Fire leaped between us. Vincent cried out and stumbled backward, his face pale.

In desperation, I grabbed the first thing I saw, a carafe half-full of last night's wine, and hurled it on the flames. When nothing remained but the smell of smoke, I whispered my apologies. "Your work. Oh, Vincent, look what I've done to your work, I've ruined it."

I reached for the charred paper, but Vincent snatched it with trembling hands. Wadding it into a ball, he threw it into a wastebasket. "It was nothing but worthless scribbling."

Horrified at what I'd done, I began to cry. "I'm sorry, I didn't mean to—"

Vincent seized my arm so tightly his nails bit through my sweater sleeve. "Go now, Cynda. I'll come to you later—by moonlight."

I left, sobbing, humiliated. The door closed softly behind me. The key turned in the lock. Sure that Vincent despised me, I ran toward the stairs, cursing myself for my clumsiness.

Too late, I saw Susan blocking my way. "What's going on? Why were you in Vincent's room?"

"Let me by." I tried to push past her, but the staircase was too narrow.

Susan forced me to face her. "You have no business being alone with a guest in his room."

"I was just talking to him. Since when is that a crime?"

She peered into my eyes, frowning as if she saw something disturbing. The anger drained out of her face. Concern took its place. "Listen to me, Cynda. Vincent is charming, handsome, sophisticated, but he's at least fifteen years older than you. For God's sake, stick to boys your own age."

"You're not my mother, you can't tell me what to do."

"I'm responsible for you," Susan said. "If you persist in hanging around Vincent's room, I'll ask him to leave the inn. I won't sit back and watch an older man seduce you."

"I suppose you'd know all about that." The words flew out of my mouth before I could stop them. "Dad must be twice your age."

Susan drew in her breath. "It was an entirely different situation. Your father—"

"You were eighteen years old," I yelled. "My mother told me all about you and Dad. You took him away from me! If it hadn't been for you—"

"What's going on?" Dad shouted from the door of his den. "How do you expect me to write?"

Without looking at me again, Susan ran downstairs toward Dad. "I need to talk to you," she said. "In private!"

The door slammed shut behind her. I stood on the steps, fists clenched, trying not to cry. I wasn't proud

103

of what I'd done, I knew I'd gone too far. But even if I'd wanted to apologize, Susan was in no mood to listen. Dad was angry too, and likely to be even angrier when she told him what I'd said.

The stairs creaked behind me. I whirled around. Vincent stood in the shadows at the top, one hand raised to keep me from running to him.

"Don't worry, Cynda," he murmured. "Susan can't come between us. Nothing can. We belong together, you and I." His voice was silky soft, no more than a whisper, laden with kindness and concern.

Silencing me with a tender smile, he vanished as quickly as he'd come. But his sympathy lingered, sweetening the still air like perfume. Vincent wasn't angry after all. As usual, he and he alone understood.

Voices rose and fell in the den. Susan and Dad were arguing. To avoid facing them, I grabbed my parka and headed for the back door. I'd go for a long walk. By the time I came back, maybe they'd be calm and rational.

Todd intercepted me in the kitchen. "Are you going somewhere with Vincent?"

Susan chose that very moment to leave the den. Luckily she was still too far away to hear Todd.

"Of course not." My voice had the ring of a lie even though I was telling the truth.

"You were with him last night," Todd said loudly.

"Hush, Toddy." Even without looking, I knew Susan heard this time. "I was in bed, sound asleep."

"I saw you, dummy." Todd made no effort to lower his voice. "You were holding his hand."

Susan came closer. "What are you talking about, Todd?"

"Cynda and Vincent went outside last night, I saw them in the snow. Tell her not to go with him again, Mommy. Tell her!"

Before Susan could say anything, I said, "Todd was dreaming. You know how he is—he can't tell the difference between what's real and what's not."

"No," Todd said, starting to cry. "Don't say that, Cynda, don't lie. I saw you."

The sight of his tears made me feel bad, but if I told the truth, Susan would send Vincent away. "I wasn't outside," I insisted. "I didn't go anywhere. Not with Vincent, not with anybody!"

Todd gave me a look of despair and threw his arms around his mother. "Vincent's making her lie," he sobbed. "She's just like him. Mean and bad and wicked."

Susan frowned at me above his head. "I don't know what to think, Cynda, but if I ever see you going anywhere with Vincent I'll make damn sure you never do it again."

I shot her a nasty look. "I'll do what I want. You can't boss me around."

With that, I ran outside and slammed the door so hard the glass rattled. It pleased me to see a flock of crows take to the air, cawing like banshees.

I looked up at Vincent's window, hoping to see him standing there, but his curtains were tightly drawn.

It was just as well. The scene with Susan had left

me weak and weepy. Turning my back on the inn, I struck out across the snow, breathing deeply, moving fast. If I walked long enough and far enough, the wind might blow my anger and hurt away.

13

Halfway to the coast, I found Vincent's and my tracks in the snow. His led toward the woods, then veered back to the inn at some distance from mine. From the look of my solitary footprints, no one had helped me. Vincent was right. I'd walked home by myself.

Still trying to understand what had happened, I studied the place where I'd fallen. Its shape reminded me of the snow angel I'd made the afternoon before Vincent arrived. With one difference—reddish-brown spots speckled the outline of my shoulders. I stared at them, puzzled. Had I injured myself? Cautiously I touched my neck. So tiny a wound, more a scrape than a cut. It couldn't have bled that much.

Uneasily I remembered the cruelty I'd glimpsed in Vincent's face, the flash of pain I'd felt when he kissed me. I shook my head to chase my fears away. Vincent wouldn't harm me. He loved me, I loved him. There must be another explanation for the drops of blood on the snow.

I thought hard. Before the wind sprang up, I'd heard an owl. Perhaps it had caught something here.

A mouse, a shrew, or some other helpless creature lost in the dark.

The wind moaned in the woods behind me and I whirled around, expecting to see the dead girl peering at me from the trees. I saw nothing, yet I was sure I heard her voice whispering again of ill, warning me, haunting me.

Unable to bear the lonely sound, I stumbled through the snow toward the ocean and took the trail down to the shore. I walked slowly beside the sea. The crash of waves and cries of gulls silenced the dead girl's sad voice. To keep from thinking about her, I found things to add to my stone and shell collection—a small piece of driftwood shaped like a bird, a glass float from a fishing net, a stone with a hole in the middle.

I was so absorbed in beachcombing I didn't notice Will until he was beside me. "I've been chasing you for five minutes," he said. "Didn't you hear me calling you?"

"Too much noise." I gestured at the waves and gulls and trudged on, head down, scuffing at stones, wishing Will hadn't happened along. I didn't feel like being polite and making conversation, pretending everything was fine. It was too much effort.

Without acknowledging my mood, Will strolled beside me, saying little. The damp, salt air curled his hair and reddened his face until he seemed to glow with health and energy. Unable to resist his warmth, I drew closer. I was cold, so cold. My fingers and toes ached, my breath iced the scarf around my neck.

Will bent to retrieve something from the surf. "Look, Cynda." He handed me a tiny scallop shell. "See the hole? You can string these and make a mermaid's necklace."

Embarrassed by the look in his eyes, I took the shell and dropped it into my pocket without saying anything. I didn't want to hurt Will. I liked him, he was nice, but he was no rival for Vincent.

Neither of us was paying any attention to the ocean. A large wave suddenly broke a few feet away. In seconds, we were knee-deep in a rough surge of cold water. To keep me from falling, Will grabbed my hand. "Come on. We can't stay here, we'll freeze."

I followed him up a steep path I hadn't noticed before. My wet jeans clung to my legs, making me slow and clumsy. At the top, the wind hit my face hard. I hoped Will knew a shortcut to the inn.

Instead of heading inland, he led me to a weather-beaten old shack not far from the edge of the cliff. He fumbled with a padlock, then shoved the door open.

"Welcome to my studio," he said, laughing at himself for giving the tumbledown building such a grand name.

While Will lit a fire in the wood stove, I looked around. The walls were covered with dark, somber watercolors, unframed, tacked up haphazardly with no attempt at symmetry. Stormy seas, cloudy skies, gulls with sharp beaks, small human figures struggling against winds and tides. They were even better than the sketches he'd drawn for Todd.

"It's okay if you don't like my pictures," he said.

109

"Grandmother says they're depressing." Without waiting to hear my opinion, he grabbed a kettle and went out to fill it with snow.

"No running water," he explained when he returned, "but we can still have tea."

We sat and took off our wet shoes and socks and set them near the stove to dry. The shack was so quiet I heard a gull cry outside, its voice as plaintive as a hungry cat's. Gusts of wind rattled the windows. Beneath the creaking and groaning of old wood, the surf rumbled. It was like being on a ship.

"This is a funny old place," I said, looking around curiously.

"Grandfather stored his fishing gear here—lobster traps, buoys, floats, nets." Will pointed at the stuff piled up behind the stove. "I moved it back there to make room to paint."

Will got to his feet and gestured for me to follow him. "Want to see something interesting?" Shoving a stack of lobster traps aside, he lifted a trapdoor. "This ladder leads to a cave. Way back in the eighteenth century, smugglers used it to hide their loot. Later it came in handy for bootleggers."

I knelt beside Will and stared into the dark. The air smelled damp and old. Far below, waves washed in and out. I shuddered and drew back. "Have you ever climbed down there?"

"Sure. It's perfectly safe. The cave is always above water, even at high tide." Will closed the trapdoor and straightened up. "You can walk out to the beach at low tide. The rocks are slippery, though. You have to be careful."

The kettle whistled then. Will opened a tin of tea bags and pawed through its contents. "Peppermint, cranberry, licorice, chamomile, and plain old Lipton —take your pick."

I chose peppermint and sipped it slowly, warming my hands with the cup. Despite the fire in the stove, my jeans were still damp from the knees down. I was cold but in no hurry to face Susan and Dad.

For a while neither Will nor I spoke, but every now and then I caught him looking at me as if he wanted to say something. His silence made me uneasy. Finally I asked him how he'd known where to find me. "Did Susan send you after me?"

Will shook his head. "I was hoping to see you when I dropped Grandmother at the inn, but you weren't there." He hesitated a moment, his face reddening with embarrassment. "Todd said you'd gone out, so I came looking for you."

I tensed, suspecting Todd had told him more than that, and waited for Will to go on.

He examined his fingernails as if he'd just noticed the paint under them. Without raising his eyes, he said, "Todd saw you with Vincent last night. He—"

"I don't care what Todd said," I interrupted. "You know what a liar he is. He's always making up stories."

"This wasn't a story, Cynda. He's scared of Vincent, he thinks—"

"Todd's scared of everything. Wolves under the bed, witches, monsters . . ." My words trailed off unconvincingly. I'd never been a good liar.

Will leaned across the table, his hands edging closer to mine. "Tell me the truth, Cynda. Did you go somewhere with Vincent last night?"

I snatched my hands away and clasped them in my lap. "Suppose I did? What business is it of yours? It's my life, I can do what I want." My voice came out louder than I'd intended. Angrier too.

Will looked at me with disapproval—or disappointment. I wasn't sure which.

"I had to lie," I went on, trying to make him understand. "If Susan knew, she'd order Vincent to leave. I'd never see him again!"

"I can't believe this," Will said. "I thought you—"

I grabbed his hands then and held them tight.

"Don't tell, Will. Promise you won't."

"Cynda, he's ten or fifteen years older than you, he's—"

I couldn't bear to listen to another word. Jumping up, I ran to the window. The ocean spread below, dull green and wrinkled under a gray sky. "Don't say anything bad about Vincent, Will. You don't know him. He's the only person in the world who cares what happens to me!"

Will followed me across the room and stopped a few inches away. "What are you talking about, Cynda? You've got your father, your stepmother, Todd—"

"That's what you think!" I whirled around and

glared at him. "Dad's got no time for me. He's always locked up in his den, writing, writing, writing those dumb books of his. And Susan—she's on my back about every little thing. I swear she hates me."

"Cynda, you can't possibly believe that."

Will's calm, reasonable voice made me madder. He was trying to talk the truth away, but I had no intention of letting him do it.

"Just look at the way they treat Todd," I shouted. "Do they ever get mad at him? Do they ever punish him? He's the one they love, not me. They brought me up here to babysit him. I'm nothing but a free au pair girl, doing this, doing that!"

I was crying now, I couldn't stop. I wanted to go back to the inn and sleep till dark. I wanted to be with Vincent. He was the only one who understood. I could be myself with him, I could tell him everything. Unlike Will, *Vincent* never criticized me, *Vincent* never looked shocked. He always agreed, he took my side.

"On top of everything else," I sobbed, "Susan's going to have *another* baby—when it's born, nobody will have any time for me at all!"

"My God, Cynda, where are you getting this crap?" Will drew in his breath, guessing. "It's Vincent, isn't it? He's really warped your mind."

"Shut up, Will! You don't know what you're talking about. You're just jealous, you said so yourself!"

That silenced him. Swearing softly, he turned his back on me and doused the fire in the stove. Then, without looking at me, he pulled on his socks and shoes. "We'd better go," he muttered. "It'll be dark soon."

"You don't need to come with me. I can find my way by myself." I yanked on my wet socks, forced my feet into wet shoes, and grabbed my parka.

"I have to go to the inn anyway," Will said. "It's time to drive Grandmother home."

We left the shack and trudged toward Underhill without speaking or looking at each other. Will's boots broke through the snow's crust every now and then, making loud crunching sounds. His nylon parka rustled.

Finally he said, "I'm sorry, Cynda. I didn't mean to make you mad. I was just trying to keep you from getting hurt. You can't trust guys like Vincent. They'll take advantage of you, they'll lie, they'll—"

"Don't worry about me." I spoke quickly to shut him up. "I can take care of myself. I'm a lot more experienced than you think."

"What's that supposed to mean?"

"Figure it out for yourself!" I walked faster, letting Will believe what he liked.

We didn't speak again till we reached the inn. In the room above mine, Vincent stood at his window, his face dimly lit by the candle on the sill. My heart sped up, pumping blood so fast my neck throbbed.

"There he is," Will muttered. "Just like a hungry cat waiting for a mouse."

Vincent smiled as if he'd heard and stepped back, letting the curtain fall. At the same moment, the

114

kitchen door opened and yellow light spilled out onto the snow.

"It's about time you came home," Susan said crossly.

Edging past her, Mrs. Bigelow hurried down the steps.

"Let's go, Will," she said, sounding almost as annoyed as Susan. "It's past five and I haven't even started dinner."

Mrs. Bigelow didn't look at me, let alone speak. She was mad at me too, I guessed. Why not? Everyone except Vincent seemed to be angry with me for one reason or another.

"Thanks for finding Cynda," Susan called after Will, but he was already in the truck, revving the motor.

When she turned to me, I said, "I wasn't lost. I just went for a walk." Without giving her a chance to say another word, I went to my room, slammed the door, and flung myself on my bed. If Susan needed help with dinner, she could ask Dad. I wasn't her servant. I wasn't Todd's nursemaid either.

Overhead, Vincent crossed the floor of his room, his step swift and light. His nearness reassured me. Susan, Dad, Todd, Will—why should I care what they thought? I had Vincent to comfort me. That was all that mattered.

14

Dinner was an ordeal of unspoken anger and resentment. Nobody said what was really wrong; we expressed our feelings indirectly. Todd, for instance, complained about his food and refused to talk to me. I was bad, he muttered, he didn't like me anymore.

Susan remonstrated with him but he slumped in his chair and kicked the table leg. That irritated Dad, who was already in a bad mood because no one liked the bouillabaisse he'd spent hours concocting. Todd choked on a fishbone, and Susan said the dish was too spicy; she'd be up all night with heartburn.

Even though Dad denied adding squid to the pot, I was sure I saw something with tentacles and tiny suction cups floating among the chunks of fish. I had no appetite anyway. It was obvious that Susan and Dad had lost patience with me. She told me to stop pouting and eat my dinner; he corrected me for saying "Can I" instead of "May I."

Before Susan took Todd up to bed, she looked at Dad in a way that made me uneasy. Hoping to avoid a scene, I started to leave the room, but Dad stopped me. "Don't rush off. I want to talk to you."

I sat down reluctantly, afraid of what was coming. "I have to study," I mumbled.

"That's one of the things we need to discuss," Dad said. "Susan tells me you've been sleeping late. She hasn't seen you crack a book for days."

"Susan doesn't know everything. I stay up past midnight studying, that's why I sleep late." I was amazed at how easily the lie rose to my lips. "I work best at night when there's nothing to distract me."

From the doorway, Susan said, "If that's true, Cynda, it might be a good idea for you to skip our evening visits with Vincent. Studying would be far more productive than sitting here gazing at him like an infatuated schoolgirl."

I stared at her, too shocked to speak. Dad drew in his breath as if he thought she'd gone too far, but Susan didn't seem to care. "It's not a healthy situation," she went on. "Your father and I think you should see less of Vincent."

When Dad nodded in agreement, I turned to him, my face burning with anger and humiliation. "Whose side are you on?" I shouted. "Hers or mine? In case you've forgotten, I'm your *daughter!*"

I expected my father to defend me, but he said, "I'm afraid I agree with Susan. We've both noticed a change in your attitude, Cynda. Although I don't think Vincent is to blame, I'm disturbed by your sneaking up to his room. Then there's Todd's story of seeing you outside with him and the nasty scene with Susan . . ." Dad fumbled with his pipe as if he were too embarrassed to go on.

I leaped to my feet. "Why did you invite me here? You never want to see me, you never talk to me about anything that matters! You lock yourself up in your den all day. Is that stupid book all you care about?"

Dad reached for my hand, but I turned and ran from the room. In the hall, I collided with Vincent.

"Cynda, what's wrong?"

His voice was rich with concern. I wanted to hurl myself into his arms and beg him to take me away. We could drive all night in his beautiful car, get married in Canada, and never return. Dad would be sorry then!

But Susan and Dad were standing a few feet away, watching, listening, forcing me to protect our secret. They mustn't guess I loved Vincent.

"Don't look so alarmed, Vince." Dad dismissed the scene with a nervous laugh. "You know how teenagers are. They have to create a little melodrama every now and then to keep themselves from getting bored."

At that moment, I hated my father. He was making a fool of me in front of Vincent, belittling my tears, turning them into a joke for adults to laugh about.

Vincent glanced at me. The little mark on my neck tingled as if he'd touched it with his lips. I knew he'd come to me later. We'd be alone, free to say and do what we wanted. Without looking at Dad or Susan, I stalked down the hall to my room.

*

Just before midnight, I heard a light footstep in the hall, then a soft rap at the door. Ebony raised his head and stared at me. Lashing his tail, he growled

118

and rose to his feet, back arched. Ignoring the cat, I tiptoed to the door.

Vincent stood in the dark hall. "May I come in?"

"Of course." I stepped aside; my heart beat hard and fast.

The moment Vincent crossed the threshold, Ebony slipped past him and ran toward the kitchen.

My room seemed smaller with Vincent in it. He prowled about, examining my books, my rocks and shells, Mom's postcards, a snapshot of her and Steve arm-in-arm in front of the Colosseum. I followed close behind, waiting for him to talk to me, hold me, kiss me.

Finally he took a seat in a chair facing the fireplace. Immediately I sat in his lap and kissed him as long as I dared. When I drew back, surprised by my own boldness, he looked hard at me. "Do you have any idea where this little game is leading, Cynda?"

Suddenly shy, I toyed with his earring. I yearned to please Vincent, to make him love me as much as I loved him. Whatever he wanted I'd give to him, he only had to ask. "I love you," I whispered into his ear, "Oh, Vincent, I love you so much."

"Do you really?" He sounded slightly amused.

"I've never loved another living soul the way I love you," I insisted. "I'd do anything for you, Vincent. *Anything*."

"Anything?" His body tensed, his eyes darkened, his amusement vanished.

I stared at Vincent, a little frightened by the change in him. The sympathy was gone from his

119

eyes, and so was the tenderness. In their place was something I'd never seen before. "Yes," I whispered. "Anything."

He twisted a strand of my hair gently around his finger. "'Bess, the landlord's daughter,'" he murmured. "'Plaiting a dark red love-knot into her long black hair.' Remember, Cynda?"

"The girl in the poem," I whispered, "the one who died to save her lover's life."

"Would you die to save my life?"

"You asked me that before," I said, trying to suppress the tiny shiver of fear racing up and down my spine. "I said I would."

"But I didn't believe you. Perhaps I should put you to the test now." Vincent rose to his feet so quickly I almost fell. Opening his arms, he said, "Come to me, Cynda."

It was a command, not an invitation. I hesitated, but he was smiling, his arms spread wide to receive me. He was certainly in no danger of dying, his life didn't need saving. Hoping it was a joke, I stepped into his arms.

"Remember, you brought this upon yourself," Vincent hissed into my ear. "It's not my nature to resist temptation."

Making no effort to deaden the pain with a kiss, he sank his teeth into my throat. Pain arced between us like electricity leaping from pole to pole. I tried to scream, tried to escape, but Vincent was too strong. He held me tightly, mercilessly. The room darkened, grew dim, spun slowly, then faster. At last I understood, I knew what Vincent was, what he wanted. Unable to bear the pain of that knowledge, I closed my eyes and prayed to die fast.

But my prayer wasn't answered. Gradually I came to my senses and found myself lying on my bed, too weak to move. Vincent sat beside me, watching me. Except for the dim light of the candles, the room was dark, silent, cold. So cold. I was numb with cold.

"Don't worry," Vincent said. "You won't die." There was no kindness in his voice, no love, no gratitude. Just a cool satisfaction.

I tried to sit up. I wanted to call my father, I needed him to protect me, but I couldn't even lift my head. Sick with fear, I stared into Vincent's eyes. "I know what you are," I whispered. "You're, you're . . ." But the word I needed was slipping away, sinking into a dark place beyond recall. I couldn't say it.

Vincent smiled. "Yes, you know, little mouse, but no one else does. Nor will you be able to tell them." Still smiling, he leaned closer. "You know what I want, too. You're willing to give it to me, aren't you? Night after night, you'll invite me to take it."

"No, no," I sobbed. "I won't let you, I won't."

Vincent touched my throat lightly, so lightly, yet my blood raced eagerly to the little red mark. His laughter broke like ice. "I've made you mine, Cynda. You can't resist me, can you?"

I turned my head, unable to bear the mockery in his eyes. "I loved you, I thought you loved me."

"Love," he said scornfully. "Poor little Cynda. Did you really believe I cared about you or your petty little problems? Such a boring litany of whining complaints—Mommy doesn't love me, Daddy doesn't love me. No one appreciates me, no one understands."

Vincent's words struck me like sharp stones. They shattered the hours I'd spent with him. They buried themselves in my heart. They annihilated everything. "Kill me," I said, weeping. "Just kill me, I don't want to live anymore."

He rose to his feet and gazed down at me as if I amused him. "Not yet," he said softly. "I'm not finished with you, my dear Cynda."

Without looking at me again, Vincent left the room. The last thing I heard was the wind's familiar lament: "Ill has come to you, ill has come."

*

I woke in the morning troubled and frightened. Scenes from books and movies tormented me, imaginary evils, things that didn't exist, couldn't exist, things I had no name for. Dreams, hallucinations . . . What I remembered couldn't be true, it hadn't happened.

When Susan came to the door, she found me in tears. "Cynda," she whispered, her face filled with concern. "What's wrong? Are you sick?"

I nodded. My throat hurt too badly to answer, but it didn't matter. Vincent had stolen the word for what he was, what he'd done. Just as he'd predicted, I couldn't tell her the truth.

Susan covered me with an extra quilt. "You'd better stay in bed. I'll bring you toast and tea."

The day passed slowly, gray and dull. Clouds hid the sun. I drifted in and out of dreams. Sometimes I saw the murdered girl hovering near me. "Ill has come to you," she sobbed. "Ill has come to me."

Sometimes Vincent came. His face hung over me, cruel and pitiless, inhuman; he whispered dark promises, he warned me not to tell. "Our secret, yours and mine; our moonlight secret; our sweet, sweet secret . . ."

At lunchtime, Susan brought me soup and a sandwich. Wrapped in his blue cape, Todd stared at me from the doorway, his face pale and worried. I heard him say something about Vincent.

"No, no, darling," Susan said. "Vincent has nothing to do with this. Cynda's sick, she has a bad cold, flu maybe."

I wanted to tell her that Todd was right, my illness had everything to do with Vincent, but she was already leading him away. "I don't want you to catch what Cynda has. It might be contagious."

Late in the afternoon, Vincent began pacing the floor above me. Back and forth, back and forth. Once his footsteps had excited me. Now they echoed dully in my head, throbbed in my veins, gave me no rest.

When Vincent came to my door tonight, I swore I wouldn't let him in. I'd call Dad, I'd make him send

Vincent away. I'd tell him exactly what sort of creature he'd invited into his home. Even if I couldn't remember the word, my father would believe me.

At least I hoped he would. Because if he didn't, if he laughed, if he said there were no such things—what would happen to me?

15

Darkness fell. The clock ticked the minutes away, chimed the hours. Every swing of the pendulum brought Vincent closer. I heard him come downstairs to have his glass of wine, I heard him go up to bed, I heard Dad and Susan follow him. The inn grew quiet. I told myself I'd be strong, I'd resist, I'd send Vincent back into the dark and the cold.

At three A.M. he came to my door. "Cynda," he called softly, "may I come in?"

The sound of his voice froze my blood. I huddled under the blankets and prayed he'd go away.

"Cynda, please let me in," he whispered. "I must talk to you, explain, apologize. I didn't mean to frighten you. I've paced the floor all day, unable to write, unable to forgive myself."

His voice ached with pain, throbbed with sadness. I felt myself weakening, but I forced myself to lie still. If I didn't get up, I couldn't open the door.

"I thought you loved me, Cynda, I thought you wanted me as much as I want you. Don't shut me out, please don't." His voice was so low I barely understood what he was saying. Vowing not to let him in, I tiptoed to the door and pressed my ear against it. I heard him breathing softly. "How can you be so cruel, Cynda?" Vincent paused as if he were struggling against his own nature. "I've never felt this way, I've never loved anyone, I didn't think I was capable of it."

I gripped the knob, wanting to believe him, yearning to be with him, to talk the way we used to. Maybe I'd been wrong, maybe I'd dreamed the horrible thing he'd done to me. It couldn't have happened the way I remembered it. It wasn't possible.

"Let me in," Vincent begged. "Just for a little while. I promise I won't hurt you."

I watched my hand turn the knob as if it belonged to someone else, I watched the door open, I heard myself say, "You can come in for a minute, but only if you . . ."

Wordlessly Vincent took me in his arms. His teeth sought my throat.

"No," I cried, "don't, please don't, you promised . . ." I pushed him, I shoved, I beat at his chest, but, like last night, I couldn't get away, couldn't even cry out. He sucked hard, greedily, drinking my blood, draining my strength.

As suddenly as he'd grabbed me, he shoved me away. I fell on the bed, weak and dizzy, and he perched beside me. His eyes shone in the dark like a cat's.

"You see?" he murmured. "I mean you no harm. I could have drained every drop of your blood, I could have killed you, but I chose not to."

"It wasn't a dream, I didn't imagine it," I sobbed.

"But you still love me."

"No," I sobbed, "I hate you, I despise you, I loathe you. You're hideous, you're depraved, vile. . . ."

Vincent listened to me curse him, smiling as if it pleased him. What I said, how I felt meant nothing to him.

"What will you do now?" he asked, twirling a strand of my hair around his finger like a ring. "You won't try to betray me, will you, Cynda?"

He tightened the ring of hair, hurting me. "Remember, you promised not to tell."

Despite the pain, I struggled to pull free of his hand, but there was no escape from his eyes. They held me, I couldn't turn away.

"Did you honestly think there'd be no price to pay for the attention I lavished on you? Even a mortal man expects a return on an investment, my dear, naive child." Releasing my hair, he lay back on my bed and gazed at me.

"Maybe I can't tell Dad everything," I whispered, "but I can at least tell him you tried to seduce me, you made advances, you took liberties, you, you . . ."

Vincent mocked my choice of words—so old-fashioned, so Victorian. "I'll tell your father *you* tried to seduce *me*," he said. "When I refused, you made up a lie to spite me."

I forced myself to sit up and slide away from him. "Dad would never take your word over mine."

But even as I spoke, I began to doubt. In all the time I'd been here, Dad hadn't once taken my side

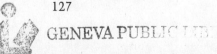

against Susan or Todd. It would be no different with Vincent. Ever since Dad had welcomed Vincent to Underhill, he'd listened eagerly to his guest's opinions. Except for his belief in ghosts, Dad agreed with every word Vincent spoke.

"After you ran to your room last night," Vincent went on, "your father told me he's thinking of taking you to a psychiatrist. He said you haven't adjusted to the divorce as well as he'd hoped. He spoke of your hostility toward Susan, your jealousy of Todd, your inability to study."

Vincent laughed and ran a finger down my cheek. His nail was just sharp enough to hurt. "Girls with emotional problems are not to be trusted, Cynda. Or believed. Besides," he chuckled, "your father thinks I'm bloody marvelous."

"I'll tell Susan, then," I said desperately.

Vincent began to play with my hair again. "Your stepmother has a small mind, full of small suspicions, but she's easily flattered. A word of praise here, a smile there, and she's mine too."

When I began to cry, Vincent yawned, showing his sharp teeth and his red tongue. "Silly little fool, don't bore me with your tears."

I raised my hands to protect my throat, but he was already at the door. "Remember, Cynda. 'I'll come to thee by moonlight, though hell should bar the way.'"

*

Several days passed. I stayed in bed till late in the afternoon, eating little, sipping tea, sleeping. Every

128

night Vincent came to my door, every night I tried to resist him, every night I failed. I had no idea what he planned to do, how long he'd let me live, or what would happen to me when I died.

One afternoon, Susan told me she was taking to me to the doctor. "It's either a bad case of flu or mononucleosis," she said, but I'd heard her whisper "Leukemia" to Dad. Or maybe bone cancer, Hodgkin's disease—words that once would have terrified me, but I knew worse things now.

I hadn't been outside for days. The wind was so cold, the light so bright it blinded me. "Please let me go back to bed," I whimpered. "Please, Susan, please."

At first it seemed I'd get my wish. The car wouldn't start. Susan swore and begged, but the engine resisted everything she did. Dad had no better luck, but instead of giving up, he called the Bigelows.

Will arrived ten minutes later. Ignoring my protests, Dad saw me off. "Take good care of her, Will."

As we pulled away from the inn, Will said, "I'm sorry you're sick, but I'm glad to have a chance to be with you. I've been wanting to patch things up. I didn't mean to make you angry last week."

I stared silently at the snowy fields and bare trees. I'd forgotten we'd quarreled. It seemed so long ago, so unimportant. I'd been a different girl then. Foolish. Stupid.

I closed my eyes and rested my head on the back of the seat. "Doesn't the sun hurt your eyes?"

"Maybe being sick makes you more sensitive to light," Will said.

Sick, oh, if only that was all it was. Then the doctor would give me medicine, advise me to rest, drink plenty of liquids. I'd get well, I'd play in the snow with Will, I'd read to Todd, everything would be the way it used to be. But there was no cure for my disease. Maybe not even death.

My neck throbbed painfully, reminding me of what I'd done in the dark with Vincent, shameful things that separated me from Will, from everyone. Things I could never tell. Things that made me despise myself. Things that bound me to Vincent's secret world forever.

By the time we got to Ferrington, the sun was low. Soon it would be replaced by the pale moon already visible just above the eastern horizon. Nightfall was near. Darkness. Vincent's time. My time.

Will stopped in front of an old brick building. Its wood trim was neatly painted. A brass knocker in the shape of a sailing ship shone on the red door. Two small evergreens flanked the stone steps.

"Do you want me to come in with you, Cynda?"

I opened the truck door. "No, of course not. I'll be okay."

He pointed up the street at a small shingled house on the corner. "That's the library. I'll wait for you there."

Leaving the truck in front of the doctor's office, Will sprinted toward the library. I walked slowly up the short path to the door and studied the brass plate on the wall. *Alvin Berman, M.D.*

I pictured the office itself—colonial furniture in the waiting room, nautical prints on the wall, a nurse in white, a jovial old doctor with a Maine accent. He'd be expecting an ordinary illness—flu, anemia, mononucleosis, whatever—but he'd encounter something he'd never studied in medical school, a condition not found in his books.

Nervously I looked behind me. Will was gone. The street was empty.

I let my breath out in a long sigh and walked away quickly. In twenty minutes I'd go to the library and meet Will. He'd never know I hadn't seen the doctor. Neither would Dad or Susan.

To escape the cold, I went to the diner and took a seat at the counter. Gina was talking to a couple of men sitting in a booth, but when she saw me, she bustled over to take my order.

"Mrs. Bigelow told me you've been sick, Cynda. How are you feeling?"

To avoid meeting her eyes, I studied the menu. "I'm okay."

"That drafty old inn is no place to spend the winter," Gina said. "I hear Todd's had a bad cold. It's a wonder the whole family's not sick."

I shuddered at the thought someone else might suffer from my disease.

She patted my hand to comfort me. "Lord, child, your fingers feel like ice. How about a nice cup of hot tea? A slice of lemon, some honey—it's sure to warm you up."

While I waited, I tried to ignore the acrid smell of brewing coffee. A hamburger sizzled and spat on the grill, a man near me puffed his cigarette, the fluorescent lights were so bright they hurt my eyes. I wanted to leave but it was cold outside and I had nowhere else to go. And I was tired, so tired. I cradled my head in my hands, too weary to move. I was lost, there was no hope for me, no help.

Gina roused me by setting a steaming cup in front of me. "Just look at the circles under your eyes," she said, obviously worried by my appearance. "And you're so pale. Are you sure you're all right?"

I shrugged, dangerously close to tears, and tried to drink my tea. My hand shook so hard I spilled some on the counter.

"Something's bothering you," Gina said slowly. "You're frightened, scared to death." Drawing a deep breath, she peered into my eyes. "It's the inn, isn't it? No matter what your father says, I swear that place is cursed."

"What do you mean?" I stared at her, wondering what she knew. Vincent's mark began to ache with a dull, throbbing pain like an abscessed tooth.

"The girl Martha told you about wasn't the first to die at Underhill," Gina whispered. "There were others before her, strange stories that scared me when I was young. I told myself you couldn't be in danger, it all happened years ago, the killers are as dead as their victims now, but . . ."

She picked up a cloth and began wiping the counter. "I just don't know what to think. There's something about that inn, what folks call an aura. It gives you a bad feeling."

I pressed my hand against my neck to ease the pain, but it didn't help. The sky was darkening. I had to get back to the inn, Vincent was waiting, soon he'd come for me.

Gina straightened up and stared at me, her eyes wide with contrition. "Lord, what's the matter with me? Now I've gone and upset you, talking nonsense like a silly old woman. I swear I haven't got the sense I was born with."

She clearly wanted me to forget what she'd told me, but I needed to know more. Any information about the inn would help. "Where did you learn all this?" I asked.

Gina returned her attention to the spot on the counter. Scrubbing vigorously, she said, "There was an article in the *Sentinel* back in 'thirty-two or 'thirty-three when they found the girl's body. One of the reporters did a story on Underhill's history and turned up the other killings."

She paused to refill a customer's coffee cup. I watched her smiling and talking to the man, maybe sharing a bit of local gossip, never dreaming the murderer she'd told me about was still very much alive. It was all I could do to sit still and drink my tea. My hands trembled, my neck throbbed, my legs and arms were weak with fear and dread. Soon I'd return to the inn. To Vincent. To darkness—and death.

133

"You can read the story yourself, Cynda." Gina was back, plump arms folded on the counter, ready to tell me more. "That's what Martha and I did. We'd heard about the murder so often we went to the library and found the newspaper article. They keep all sorts of old stuff there."

Once more, she patted my hand. "You look so tired, Cynda. Go on home, get some rest. For the Lord's sake, take care of yourself."

I left the diner without looking back. *Take care of myself*—if only I could.

16

Outside the diner, I leaned against a telephone pole and waited for my heart to slow down. When I felt strong enough, I walked toward the library. Except for a lurid streak of crimson on the western horizon, purple clouds darkened the sky. The moon hid her face. Most of the stars kept her company.

The wind nipped at my heels and bit through my parka. Overhead, branches swayed and creaked. Street lights cast dancing shadows on the snow's icy crust. Across the road, a child came to a window and peered out. Behind her a woman moved to and fro, setting a table. A man read the evening paper. I raised a hand in greeting. Giving me one long, lingering look, the child turned away. Someone pulled a blind and the curtain fell, separating me from the little girl.

I exhaled slowly. My breath drifted away like smoke. I hurried into the library, anxious to escape the cold.

I found Will at a reading table, so deeply immersed in a book he didn't notice me till I cleared my throat.

He looked up. "You're back sooner than I thought. What did Dr. Berman say?"

"I'm just run-down," I said, unable to meet his eyes. "A little rest and I'll be fine."

"That's great." Getting to his feet, Will began to gather his books, but I stopped him.

"If you don't mind, I want to look for something." When he offered to help, I told him to stay where he was. "I can find it by myself."

Will shrugged and sat down. His red cheeks suggested my voice had been sharper than I'd intended.

It took longer than I'd thought. The old newspapers were on microfilm. I had to spool through several reels from the thirties before I saw the headline I wanted: "Missing Girl's Body Found Near Underhill Inn." The type was blurry and hard to read. If I kept Will waiting too long he might come looking for me. I didn't want him to see what I was doing. He might ask questions I couldn't answer.

Feeding coins into the machine, I made a copy of the story. Then, without reading them, I folded the pages, slipped them into my purse, and told Will I was ready to leave.

As we left the building, he took my hand. I clung to his hand, loving its warmth, its ordinariness. For a second, I felt like a normal person, a girl walking down a street with a boy, listening to him talk about school assignments and tests, familiar, everyday things.

Then I remembered Vincent and the hours of darkness that lay ahead. Gently I freed my hand from Will's and climbed into the truck. If only I had the courage to tell him what was really wrong with me. If only he could help me.

When we pulled into the inn's parking lot, the porch light flashed on, and Dad opened the back door. Waving to Will, he invited him to have dinner with us. "Susan's set a place for you."

Will shook his head, but Dad insisted. It was the least he could do to thank him for taking me to the doctor. "I've got steaks ready for the grill."

"You can't say no," Susan added. "We've already phoned your grandmother. If you don't eat here you won't eat anywhere."

Will threw up his hands in surrender and followed me inside. Todd was delighted to see him. Ignoring me, he begged Will for a piggyback ride. As they galloped out of the room, I heard Todd say something unpleasant about me.

Susan heard too. Looking up from the tray she was preparing for Vincent, she said, "Todd doesn't mean it, Cynda. Children go through stages. Before you know it, he'll be crazy about you all over again."

I watched her carry the tray out of the kitchen. She probably thought she was disappointing me by taking it upstairs herself. Little did she know the last thing I wanted now was to be alone with Vincent.

When Susan returned, she asked what Dr. Berman had said. I was standing at the window, my back to her, staring at the snowman Will, Todd, and I had made weeks ago. He was thinner now and brittle with ice. His face reminded me of Vincent's.

Without looking at Susan, I repeated the lie I'd told Will. "I'm just run-down."

"Did you have some blood work done?" she asked.

I nodded. No lie this time. I'd certainly had blood work done.

"I have a feeling you're anemic," Susan said. "When Dr. Berman gets the test results, he'll probably prescribe iron supplements."

I smiled to myself. Anemic, yes, I was no doubt anemic. My blood needed more than iron, though. Without a transfusion, I'd soon be as white and bloodless as the snowman.

I watched Susan's reflection in the window. She moved about the kitchen purposefully, maneuvering her stomach around obstacles, her attention fixed on preparing a salad. How innocent she seemed, how pure and untouched by evil. What would she say if I whirled about and told her the truth?

"By the way," I might say, "Vincent comes to my room late at night and sucks my blood, that's why I'm sick. What do you think we should do about it?"

Even if I dared tell her, Susan wouldn't believe me. Worse yet, Vincent would kill me for betraying him. Weeks from now, some poor soul would find my body washed up on the rocks.

Dad came into the kitchen, carrying a platter of freshly grilled steaks. "Dinner is served," he announced.

Unwillingly I took my place at the table, hemmed in like a prisoner between Will and Dad. The smell of food made my head ache, the sound of chewing and swallowing sickened me. I pictured the digestive system as shown in my ninth grade science book, remembered the dry explanation of what happened in the stomach and intestines.

Dad leaned toward me. "Eat your steak, Cynda. Red meat is just what you need to build up your strength."

I stared at the meat, cooked extra rare the way I liked it. Red juices seeped out and puddled on the plate. Without thinking, I lowered my head and licked the juice, recognizing it for what it was— blood.

"Cynthia!" Dad reached for my plate. "What are you doing?"

Suddenly angry, I tipped the plate and drank more of the blood before Dad could stop me.

Todd covered his face and began to cry. Horrified by my behavior, Susan lifted him out of his chair and left the room.

Dad stared at me. Beside him, Will sat stupefied, his mouth open.

Realizing what I'd done, I pushed the plate away and burst into tears. Dad took my arm. "You're over-tired, Cynda. You'd better go to bed, lie down, get some rest."

Too ashamed to look at Will, I left the room with my father. At my door, Dad stopped and studied my face. "Why did you do that, Cynda? What in God's name is wrong with you?"

I clung to him. "I must be crazy," I sobbed. "Maybe you should take me to the hospital, lock me up in the psych unit, keep me there."

Dad stroked my hair and murmured comforting words. I was sick, visiting Dr. Berman had exhausted me, I'd feel better in the morning, and so on and so on. "Get into bed, Cynda, rest."

"Don't leave me, Daddy," I begged. "Stay with me, don't let him come, keep him away."

Dad freed himself from my hands. "Keep who away? What are you talking about?"

I fell on my bed weeping. I couldn't say Vincent's name. He was right over my head, pacing back and forth. His footsteps beat out a warning: *Don't tell, keep it a secret, remember your promise*.

"Nothing," I sobbed, "nothing, I'm just upset, I don't know what I'm saying. Just stay a while, please, Daddy."

Dad sighed and sat down on the bed. "I left poor Will sitting at the table all by himself," he said. "And Susan's worried about you, I have to tell her you're all right."

"Please, Daddy, please." I clung to his hand and cried like a baby. I hadn't been this upset since he'd left Mom years ago. I'd begged him to stay with us, I'd wept, I'd promised to be good, but he hadn't listened then and he wasn't listening now.

"Cynda, for heaven's sake, you're sixteen years old, you're in your own room, what on earth can happen to you?"

I heard the impatience in Dad's voice, but I kept on pleading. In desperation, I used my ultimate weapon. "You don't love me," I sobbed. "You never have."

140

"That's ridiculous." Dad stood up and went to my door. "Get a grip on yourself, Cynda. I mean it. There's no reason for this behavior."

He left, shutting the door firmly behind him. I listened to his footsteps march away. I started to run after him but stopped at my door. Will was still in the dining room; I heard his voice. I couldn't face him.

The ceiling creaked. Vincent kept pacing, his ear attuned to every sound from below. Soon he'd come downstairs. Taking his seat in the shadows, he'd charm Dad and pacify Susan. Then, when they were fast asleep, he'd come to my room. Even as I vowed to keep him out, I knew I wouldn't be able to. He'd taken too much of my strength.

*

Hours later, Vincent tapped on the door. "Cynda," he whispered, "let me in."

I tried to ignore him but his voice sang in my veins and throbbed in my neck. Moving like a sleepwalker, I opened the door and Vincent stepped into my room.

When he'd taken what he wanted, he lay on the bed beside me. I gazed into his eyes, so alien, so cold. It was hard to focus. His face seemed to double, triple, and split into dozens of replicas. Finally I succeeded in making him stay still. One Vincent was more than enough.

Propping himself up on his elbow, he said, "Shall I tell you about myself, Cynda? I know you're curious.

141

Mortals love to hear my history. They find it fascinating."

I closed my eyes. Vincent's ego was boundless. He'd tell me whether I wanted to hear or not.

"I've been as I am for over five hundred years," he began. "The immortal who gave me his blood was a master of the species. Like him, I cannot be stopped with garlic, silver crosses, or stakes through the heart. I dislike sunlight, but it cannot seriously harm me. Nor do I need a coffin of earth to sustain me. Why should I? I've never been buried."

He chuckled and ran his finger down my throat, caressing the mark he'd made. "Some of my brothers and sisters claim they were taken against their will. They insist they despise themselves, they long to die. Not I. I sought my destiny, I yearned for it. I have no wish to end my life. I'm delighted with myself."

Somewhere in the darkness, the owl called. Vincent sprang to his feet and flung the window open to listen. When the last spooky note faded away, he turned to me and smiled. "How I love this old inn. It suits my needs perfectly—lonely, isolated, far from town, near the sea."

Cautiously I slid off the bed. My legs were weak, my head so light I feared I might float across the snow as weightless as smoke.

Vincent slid his arm around my waist to steady me. "Best of all," he murmured in my ear, "whenever I return to Underhill, I find a tender little mouse waiting for me, eager to give me what I need."

He pointed into the darkness. The murdered girl

stood on the snowy lawn, gazing at us and weeping. There were others with her, paler and less substantial, some no more than glimmerings of moonlight. Like her, they wept.

"My fans," Vincent said, scorning them. "Even though their bodies are dust, they still want me." He raised his hand in a threatening gesture and the ghosts fled, dissolving like mist. "They dare not come near."

"And will you kill me too?" I whispered.

Vincent smiled. "The choice is yours, Cynda. As long as you amuse me, why should I kill you?"

He closed the window then and led me back to bed. Tossing a quilt over me, he stretched out beside me. "I've been careless of your health," he said, "so careless, your friend Will drove you into Ferrington to see a doctor."

"I didn't go in, I couldn't, I thought he might. . ."

Vincent cut me off with an unpleasant chuckle. "A doctor would indeed be puzzled by your blood."

I stared at him. "You're doing something to me, aren't you? You're changing me, I'm not the same. The sun hurts my eyes, I can't concentrate, I do strange things, the whole world seems different, darker, scarier. . ."

"It's unavoidable," he admitted. "When I take your blood, my saliva enters your veins. It affects your behavior, your appetite, your response to sunlight." He laughed. "I'm an infection for which there is no cure. Not even death."

I shrank away from him. "No wonder Todd hates

me. I'm becoming more and more like you, and he knows it."

"What a clever little devil the child is." Vincent rolled over on his back and contemplated the ceiling. I watched him uneasily, wishing I could read his thoughts as easily as he read mine.

Suddenly he laughed out loud and sprang to his feet, obviously pleased with himself. Before he left, he leaned down to embrace me. "'One kiss, my bonny sweetheart,'" he whispered, "'I'm after a prize tonight.'"

I pulled away, fearing the sharp teeth behind his lips.

"Such a fickle child," he said. "Once you couldn't get enough of my kisses."

Not long after the door closed behind him, I heard a soft cry. It might have been the owl, it might have been the cat, it might have been almost anything. Yet I found it hard to sleep for worrying. Was Vincent merely quoting a line of poetry or did he plan to seek another victim?

17

Susan shook me awake. "You frightened me, Cynda. You were sleeping so soundly, you didn't move, I wasn't even sure you were breathing. I thought . . ."

She didn't need to finish the sentence, I knew what she thought. In fact, I almost wished it were true. Let the game end, let him stop, grow tired, finish me.

"How do you feel?"

I shut my eyes against the sunlight. My head throbbed, my throat hurt. I felt thinner, smaller, lighter. If it weren't for the covers anchoring me to the bed, I'd surely float away like milkweed fluff in the autumn wind.

"Maybe I shouldn't have disturbed you, maybe I should have let you sleep." Susan gestured at the tray she'd set on the table. "But I thought you should eat something."

I shook my head. "I'm not hungry."

"Please, Cynda, just a sip of tea." Susan held the cup toward me.

Steam rose, bringing with it the scent of peppermint. I closed my eyes, reminded of Will and the day he'd fixed tea in his studio. Will, kind, sweet, normal Will. He'd stayed for dinner last night, he'd sat beside me, he'd seen me lap the steak's juice like an animal. I'd frightened my little brother, I'd horrified and disgusted everyone—including myself.

"Last night," I whispered, "what I did, it was awful, terrible—" Unable to go on, I covered my face with my hands and wept.

Susan patted my shoulder. "Jeff shouldn't have insisted you eat. You were tired, upset . . ." Her voice trailed off. She'd run out of excuses.

"But Will," I said, "Will must think . . ."

Susan shook her head. "He understands, Cynda."

Silently I finished the sentence for her. *Will understands you're crazy.*

"Don't cry," she said. "You'll waste your strength."

Strength, I had no strength. Vincent had taken it all. I looked at Susan, but she was staring at the doorway where Todd had suddenly appeared.

"I thought I told you to stay in bed today," she said wearily. "Your cold is worse. You need to rest."

Instead of leaving, Todd climbed onto my bed and rested his head against Susan's stomach. "When the new baby comes, you won't love me anymore," he said sadly. "I'll be all alone."

"Where did you get such a silly idea?" Susan asked, taking Todd's unhappiness as lightly as Dad would have.

Todd began to cry. "There's nothing silly about it."

Susan stroked his blond curls. "You're not all

146

alone, Todd. Daddy loves you and so do I. The baby won't change anything."

He shook his head. "That's not what *he* says."

Susan stared at Todd, puzzled. "Surely you don't mean your father?"

"No, not Daddy," Todd said scornfully. "Daddy lies just like you."

"What are you talking about?" Susan grabbed Todd's shoulders and peered into his eyes.

"He came in my room last night, he told me things—"

At that moment, Vincent began to pace back and forth on the floor above. Todd stared at the ceiling and drew in his breath. "I was just teasing, Mommy. Nobody told me that, I made it up."

Wriggling away from his mother, Todd slid close to me. "Vincent's my friend now," he whispered. "He likes me better than you, he told me so."

Without hearing what he'd said, Susan took Todd's hand. "Back to bed, sweetie. Maybe you'll feel better tonight."

Long after they were gone, I lay still and listened to Vincent's footsteps. Now I knew where he'd gone after he left me, whose cry I'd heard in the dark, what prize he'd been after. Why had I told Vincent about Todd? Sick with guilt, I swore I'd save my brother—if I could. The ease with which Vincent had taken him frightened me.

When I felt strong enough to get up, I read the newspaper article I'd copied at the library. The murdered girl's name was Eleanor Dunne. She'd died in 1934 at the age of sixteen. A blurred photograph showed a pretty face, sweet and shy. A yearbook pose, a yearbook smile.

According to the reporter, Eleanor was a quiet, studious girl. Her parents, the owners of Underhill Inn, had no idea she'd fallen in love with a guest, a man they'd admired and trusted. A gentleman, Mrs. Dunne said of Victor McThane; intelligent and well educated, a good conversationalist, Mr. Dunne said.

Goose bumps prickled my arms—if Vincent killed me, Dad and Susan would say just what Eleanor's parents had said.

I forced myself to go on reading. Apparently Eleanor had made it a practice to meet Victor secretly. One cold night, someone saw her walking arm-in-arm with him on the cliff top. The next morning her parents found her bed empty. Several days later, three fishermen found Eleanor's corpse on the rocks, her throat slashed, her body drained of blood and white as snow.

The police looked for McThane, but he had disappeared without a trace. To aid in the search, an artist had drawn a crude sketch of the man. It didn't surprise me to see Vincent's face staring at me from the old newspaper. He and Victor were one and the same.

Accompanying the account of Eleanor Dunne's murder was another story titled "A History of Violent Deaths at Old Inn." In Underhill's early days, smugglers and criminals frequented the place, brawling and killing one another, but the reporter felt a disproportionate number of young women had been slain there. One every sixty years or so. None of the murders had been solved, yet the method was always the same. The victim's throat was slashed and her body was thrown into the sea.

"Legend has it that Underhill is haunted," the story concluded. "Perhaps there is good reason to believe the legend."

I refolded the paper carefully and slipped it into my pocket. Vincent had told the truth. He'd been coming to Underhill since it was built, letting enough time pass between visits to ensure no one would recognize him when he returned. How was I to save Todd and myself from such a powerful killer?

A draft stirred the curtains. For a second, icy fingers touched my face. "Ill come to him," Eleanor sighed, "ill come to him."

I reached out, longing for her help, but Susan chose that moment to open my door. Eleanor vanished, leaving nothing behind but cold salt air.

"It's freezing in here," Susan said, shivering. "Why don't you come sit by the fire with us?"

I followed her down the hall and stopped in the living-room doorway, horrified. Todd perched on Vincent's knee, a book spread open on his lap. Dad sat nearby, reading the evening paper. Susan took a seat beside him and picked up her sewing. Only Ebony remained aloof.

"And what did the little piggie say when he heard the big bad wolf at the door?" Vincent asked Todd.

Todd gazed at Vincent adoringly. "The little piggie

said, 'Come in, Mr. Big Bad Wolf. I'm not scared of you.'"

Over my brother's head, Vincent smiled, daring me to betray him. I stared into his eyes, more afraid of his strength than ever before.

"Why, here's Cynda," he said in that deep voice I'd once found so charming. "I'm delighted you feel well enough to join us."

Without looking at Vincent, I crossed the room and took a seat on the couch beside my father. I wanted to warn Dad, but there was nothing I could say, nothing I could do.

"Look at Todd," Dad said fondly. "It's the funniest thing, but all of a sudden, he can't get enough of Vince. I knew he'd warm up to him sooner or later."

When Vincent began tickling Todd, I leaned close to whisper in Dad's ear. "Do you think it's a good idea for Todd to get that excited? He has a cold, maybe a fever, I think he should be in bed."

Dad shrugged. "There's no harm in his having a little fun."

A few minutes later Susan called us to the dining room. Dinner was ready and Vincent was joining us. Todd insisted he sit next to him.

I watched Vincent closely. He ate little, if anything, yet he managed to get rid of his food. I suspected he slid it into his lap and concealed it in his napkin, but I never actually saw him do it. He was very quick, very clever.

More than once Vincent caught me staring at him.

150

His eyes danced with malice. He had a new game now. Two mice instead of one.

"Eat your dinner, Todd," Susan begged. "You too, Cynda."

We looked at each other, Todd and I. We weren't hungry. We had no appetite.

When Todd's bedtime came, he begged Susan to let Vincent take him upstairs. "I want Vincent to put me to bed, I want Vincent to tell me stories."

I stared at Susan. "No," I whispered, "no."

She didn't hear me. No one did except Vincent. Unseen by the others, he raised his eyebrows mockingly. There was nothing I could do to stop him. Dumb as a stone, I watched him hoist Todd onto his shoulders and carry him away.

Dad smiled at Susan. "Will better watch out. If he's not careful, he'll lose his hero's crown to Vincent."

"Vincent has developed a wonderful rapport with Todd," Susan agreed.

I listened silently, fearing for them, for Todd, for me. Blinded by Vincent's dark spell, my father and stepmother saw no danger, sensed no evil. They couldn't protect Todd and me. They couldn't protect themselves. We were all at Vincent's mercy. He was free to destroy us if he wished.

Fear swept through my veins, cold and strong. I had to do something. Or at least try. Vincent had been upstairs for half an hour. That was time enough for him to hurt Todd.

Leaving Dad and Susan at the table, I forced

myself to climb the steps to the third floor. Todd's room was at the end of the hall, just above Vincent's. A narrow band of light shone under the closed door. Slowly and cautiously, I crept near to listen, but all was silent.

"Come in, Cynda," Vincent called softly.

I opened the door. Vincent cradled Todd on his lap. My brother's head lolled back, exposing his white throat. His eyes were closed, his body limp.

I sagged against the bed, nauseated. The resentment I'd once felt for Todd melted away at the sight of his helplessness.

"Don't," I whispered, "please, Vincent, please don't. He's just a little boy."

Vincent laid Todd down and covered him with his blue blanket. "Don't worry, Cynda, I didn't take much. You'll have your chance later."

I wanted to go to Todd, but Vincent turned out the light and ushered me into the hall. "What's done is done, Cynda. There's nothing you can do for Todd now. Or yourself."

Soundlessly he descended the stairs behind me, calling out to Dad that Todd was asleep, he'd settled right down without a murmur of protest.

"A sweet boy," he whispered in my ear, "quite delicious."

18

Dad was surprised to see me come downstairs with Vincent. "I thought you'd gone to your room, Cynda."

I ran to his side, but Vincent's eyes silenced me. "I just wanted to say good night to Todd," I mumbled.

From the way Susan looked at me, I knew she thought I'd followed Vincent upstairs to be alone with him. She seemed pleased that he'd thwarted me by coming down so promptly. Obviously he hadn't encouraged me. That must mean she had nothing to worry about after all. I was safe with Vincent, we all were.

"Why don't you go to bed, Cynda," she suggested. "The inn's drafty, I don't want you to get chilled."

I turned to Dad. "Let me stay with you for a while. I feel better, honestly I do."

At that moment the doorbell rang. The sound startled us all. "Who could that be?" Susan asked.

Dad opened the door. Will stood on the threshold. The wind entered with him, shrieking as it fled past us.

"I was on my way home," he said. "I thought I'd drop in to see how Cynda is."

I glanced at Vincent. He was staring thoughtfully at Will, his face guarded, his body tense, as wary as a cat when a dog enters a room. When he caught me watching him, he smiled and stretched out his hand to Will. "Nice to see you again," he said cordially. "How's the painting coming?"

Will avoided shaking Vincent's hand by turning away to hang up his jacket. "Fine," he mumbled.

The five of us went into the living room. I sat on the couch near the fire, and Will dropped down beside me, so close his shoulder touched mine. I heard the blood run in his veins, I heard his heart pump. He was warmer than the fire, better. I slid nearer, fascinated by his jugular. I longed to kiss it, bite it, taste the sweet, red liquid pulsing through it.

Across the room, Vincent cleared his throat. My eyes met his and he winked. He knew why I'd moved closer to Will, he knew what I wanted. Poor Will had no idea.

Horrified by my own desires, I moved to the other end of the couch. I didn't trust myself. I was sick, infected, diseased. No one was safe from me.

Will seemed disappointed by the distance I'd put between us, but he didn't say anything. Except for Vincent, no one else noticed. Susan's head was bent over her sewing, and Dad was engrossed in telling Will about a problem he was having with the inn's antiquated plumbing. How could he and Susan sit in the presence of evil and suspect nothing?

Suddenly Vincent leaned toward Will. "I'd like to see your paintings. I have some contacts in the

154

city. Perhaps I could help you sell some of your work."

He rose and walked across the room to Will. "Here's my card. Give me a call when I return to New York. Or come see me. You'll always be welcome. The art world is in need of new blood."

Vincent glanced at me, relishing his joke.

Will took the card and studied it. Without looking at Vincent, he thanked him and slipped the card into his shirt pocket.

"Isn't that lovely, Will?" Susan smiled approvingly. "Think what it would mean to have your work on display in a posh New York gallery."

Dad agreed. "What a great thing to do, Vince. Will needs encouragement. He's too shy to go out and promote himself."

I watched Will carefully, waiting to see if Vincent's flattery might work this time. Perhaps Will, too, would fall under our guest's dark spell. I'd have no one then. No one but Vincent.

Will examined a loose thread in his sweater but said nothing. Susan must have noticed he was uncomfortable. "Why don't you kids go out to the kitchen and make popcorn for us? I'd do it myself, but I'm feeling lazy tonight."

In the kitchen, I avoided getting close to Will. He was so innocent, so trusting. He had no fear of me, didn't dream he was in danger.

I picked up a pot, but my hands shook so badly I dropped it. Will bent to retrieve it, exposing the tender nape of his neck. My teeth chattered like

Ebony's when he saw a bird at the feeder. I backed away.

Will stared at me. "What's wrong, Cynda?"

"Don't come any closer," I whispered. "Stay away from me."

He frowned. "What do you think I'm going to do?"

"Just go home, Will," I begged. "Don't come here anymore. Don't call Vincent, either—tear up his card, burn it."

When I started crying, Will reached out for me. "Cynda," he whispered, "Cynda, what's wrong?"

I trembled in his arms. His neck was so close, my lips were touching his jugular vein, the blood was right there, singing to me. One quick bite and it was mine. Overcome with horror, I tried to push him away.

"You don't know what I'm becoming," I sobbed. "I'm evil, wicked. Believe me, Will, I'm not fit to be near you or anyone else."

Will stared at me. "It's Vincent, isn't it? He's done something to you."

My silence confirmed his suspicions. "That bastard. I knew he'd hurt you. I warned you, Cynda, I told you he was no good."

I still said nothing. If Will knew what I'd let Vincent do, he'd despise me as much as I despised myself.

Will drew in his breath. "You're afraid of him. Has he threatened you in some way?"

Unable to bear his concern, I covered my face and wept. Immediately he drew me close again and held me tight, hoping to comfort me. "You're shaking with fear," he murmured. "My God, Cynda, what has he done to you?"

"This," I sobbed, "this." I pressed my teeth against Will's neck, then jerked my head away without breaking the skin, without tasting the blood.

Will's hand flew to his neck, covering the tooth-marks I'd left. His eyes filled with shock.

I pulled the newspaper article out of my pocket and thrust it at him. "Hide this, read it later. Don't let Vincent see it."

Watching me warily, Will buttoned the folded papers into his shirt pocket. Behind him, Vincent appeared in the doorway. Will must have sensed his nearness. He turned to face him, keeping his body between Vincent and me.

"Susan sent me to inquire about the popcorn." Vincent looked at the pot on the table and the unopened package beside it. "It appears you haven't even begun."

Will shrugged and put his arm around me. "Cynda and I were enjoying a little time together."

Vincent's reaction took us both by surprise. Without warning, he sprang on Will and wrestled him to the floor. The noise brought Dad and Susan to the door.

"Help me," Vincent yelled at Dad. "He was trying to rape your daughter!"

"No, no," I whispered. "Don't believe him, Dad, he's lying." My father paid no attention. I couldn't speak loud enough to make him hear me.

157

"Let me go!" Will broke free from Vincent only to be grabbed by Dad. "He's lying, Mr. Bennett. Guard Cynda against him, not me!"

Dad stared at Will, unsure what to believe.

"Your daughter was trying to defend herself," Vincent said. "Look at his neck. See the toothmarks? He's obviously not the sort of boy who takes no for an answer."

"Mr. Bennett, Mrs. Bennett." Will turned desperately from Dad to Susan, pleading to be believed. "You know me, surely you don't think I'd hurt Cynda."

"Why would Vincent lie?" Dad asked Will. His voice shook with hurt. Someone he'd trusted had betrayed him. Was it Will or Vincent?

Susan put her arm around my shoulders. "What happened, Cynda? Tell me."

"Yes," Will cried. "For God's sake, Cynda, tell her. Say something!"

But Vincent was staring at me, mocking me, silencing me with his eyes. "Please," he murmured, "don't pressure Cynda. She's ill, weak, she may faint."

As he spoke, the kitchen spun, faces whirled, voices ran together, and everything went black.

*

When I opened my eyes, I was in bed. Susan and Dad bent over me. "Will," I whispered, "Will . . ."

"Don't worry," Dad said wearily. "He's gone. I told him he was no longer welcome here." He covered my hand with his. "I trusted Will, I never dreamed he'd behave like this."

"Drugs," Susan murmured. "He must have taken something. It's the only explanation."

I shook my head, unable to say more. Vincent stood behind Dad and Susan, watching me intently, his lips curved in a mocking smile.

Dad smoothed the quilt over me. "Rest now," he said. "You've had a terrible shock. We all have."

I wanted to beg Dad to stay, but I remembered what had happened the last time. I'd only irritated him. Now I was too weak to make the effort, wasn't even sure I could speak—not with Vincent staring at me.

Dad gave me a hug and left the room with Susan. Vincent lingered long enough to blow me a swift kiss. Then the door closed and I lay alone in the dark, dreading his return.

19

Hours later, Vincent's knock woke me. "Cynda," he whispered. "Cynda, open the door."

Todd giggled. "Little Pig, Little Pig," he called softly. "Let us come in."

Totally defeated, I went to the door. Todd smiled down at me from his perch on Vincent's shoulders, his eyes dark with mischief. A tiny red mark like mine was barely visible just above his pajama collar. From the look on my brother's face, it seemed Vincent had bent him completely to his will.

"Oh, Toddy," I whispered, stricken by the change in him. "Why aren't you in bed? Dad and Susan would be so mad if they knew you were here."

"You'd better not tell," Todd said fiercely. "Vincent says I can stay up late and do whatever I please. I don't have to do what Daddy says anymore. Or Mommy either. Only sillies sleep at night."

Vincent lowered Todd to the floor. "Your half brother is amazingly cooperative," he said. "A quick learner, a pleasure to teach. You could benefit from his example, Cynda dear."

Todd ran to my window and began to play with the rocks and shells I'd arranged on the sill. I watched him move them about, giving them names and personalities. Absorbed in his game, he seemed totally unaware of what was happening to us.

I grabbed Vincent's arm. "What have you done to him? He used to hate you. He wouldn't come near you and now look at him!"

Vincent pulled away and smoothed his sweater sleeve. "Sometimes those who hate me on sight are the ones most attracted to me. They make the best pupils."

For a moment, he watched Todd. A smile twitched the corners of his mouth, but it lacked the strength to reach his cold, dark eyes.

Todd must have sensed Vincent's gaze because he turned to show him a large stone, one of my favorites, a perfect pale-green egg shape. "Watch this," he shouted. "It's a bomb." He dropped the rock on a pile of small shells, including the tiny scallop Will had given me. "Boom, boom, everyone's dead!"

Todd laughed happily when Vincent smiled at him. It was obvious my brother hungered for his new friend's approval.

Vincent turned back to me. "It's so simple, Cynda. All I had to do was play upon his fears and petty little jealousies. Now he thinks I'm the only one who understands him, the only one who loves him. Without me, he'd be all alone."

It was just what he'd done to me. My face flushed

with shame, and Vincent laughed. "My approach works every time, doesn't it? You're so pitifully predictable, so easy to win over."

Still chuckling, he flung himself down on my bed. "Come here, Cynda. Tell me about your wicked stepmother and your cold, unloving papa. Let me kiss your tears away, my poor, sweet darling."

When I refused, he reached out, grabbed my wrist, and pulled so hard I sprawled beside him.

Todd immediately ran to join us. "Let me play too, let me," he insisted, desperately afraid of being left out.

Vincent made room for him. Cuddling us close, he said, "Up till now, I've never shared my immortality, never given my blood, never reproduced. I've enjoyed my solitude and my freedom, but after so many years I find myself questioning my selfish existence. Perhaps it's time to grow up and take some responsibility. It might improve my character to raise a son and daughter. To be a family man."

He paused to kiss Todd, who was tumbling over us, nipping our fingers with sharp teeth. I reached for my brother, but Vincent squeezed my wrist till I almost cried with pain.

"Think of it, Cynda," he murmured. "A widowed father with two charming children, living in an elegant apartment in Manhattan. We'll mingle with the wealthiest people in the city, go to parties, the theater, symphonies, ballets. You'll have your pick of eligible young men. Todd will have all the playmates he desires. And I—" Vincent sighed with anticipation. "I'll continue to find my pleasure in the usual ways."

He caressed my face, smoothed my hair, smiled lovingly into my eyes. "If you become mine, Cynda, you'll never die, never grow old, never be in pain. Instead of weakening as mortals do, you'll grow stronger and lovelier as the years pass. No wrinkles will mar your face, no gray will dull your hair. As you are now, you will be forever."

His voice had dropped so low it sang in my blood, conjuring up pictures of myself pale and hauntingly beautiful, dressed in black velvet, bedecked with jewelry, a creature of power and beauty, a woman men would die for.

The red mark on my neck throbbed in rhythm with my heart. I moved closer to Vincent, yearning for the quick touch of his teeth and the transformation he promised.

Vincent smiled, his lips parted, his teeth gleamed. "What do you say, Cynda? Will you be my little girl forever? I promise I'll be a good father, endlessly understanding and loving. I'll never leave you, never love anyone better than you."

"Don't forget me," Todd whimpered. "You promised I could be your little boy, you promised you'd love *me* best, you said no baby would come along and ruin everything."

"Of course I won't forget you, Toddy." Vincent hugged my brother, watching me as he did so. "You'll be my favorite son and Cynda will be my favorite daughter. I'll love you both the same."

Todd frowned at me as if he were reluctant to share Vincent with anyone.

"I'll let you stay up all night long," Vincent told him. "I'll never get cross or spank you. You can eat whatever you want, whenever you want. I'll buy you toys, books, even a pony if you like."

He held Todd closer. "You know what?" he whispered. "If you decide you want a new mother, I'll let you choose one."

"And she won't have a baby?"

"Not unless you want her to."

Todd sighed and lifted his face. "Kiss me, Vincent. I like how your teeth feel."

Vincent nuzzled Todd's neck. The sight shattered the images of bliss he'd conjured up so skillfully. I saw him clearly. I remembered what he was. The price Todd and I would pay for the life Vincent promised was too high, too bloody, too horrible.

With the last of my strength, I flung myself at Vincent and pounded him with my fists. "No," I cried. "No! Take me, not Todd!"

Vincent raised his head and smiled. "Don't be so impatient, Cynda. You must wait your turn like a good little girl."

"Yes, Cynda," Todd said, smiling drowsily. "I'm first."

While Vincent busied himself with my brother, I lay still, defeated. The wind sobbed at the window. Eleanor was outside in the dark, cold and frightened. Had Vincent promised her and the other girls eternal life too?

164

"Don't cry, Cynda," Vincent murmured, turning to me. The last thing I saw was the moon. Pale and pocked as old snow, it gazed through my window, unutterably sad and weary.

*

The next afternoon, I forced myself to get out of bed, dress, comb my hair—ordinary things I used to do without thinking, without effort. Now it seemed to take all my strength to pull a sweater over my head.

There was no sound from Vincent's room, but when I walked into the hall, I heard the familiar noise of Susan's sewing machine and Dad's printer. As usual, the two of them were shut away in their own little worlds.

I thought Todd might be asleep, but I found him alone in the living room, sitting on the floor and staring at nothing, his face pale and expressionless. His toys lay scattered on the rug beside him.

He didn't notice me till I knelt beside him. "What are you thinking about, Toddy?"

"Nothing."

I touched his shoulder. Instead of drawing away as I feared he might, he nestled a little closer. "We played too much last night," he said. "I'm all tired out."

"Me too." I hesitated a moment. "Maybe it's not good for us to stay up so late, Todd. Maybe it's making us sick."

He pulled back to frown at me. "Vincent wouldn't do anything bad, he loves us, he said so. I'm his little boy and you're his little girl."

I took a deep breath. "You mustn't believe everything Vincent tells you, Todd. He doesn't, he can't, he . . ." I couldn't say what I wanted to say, the words slipped away, my mind felt muddled, my tongue thick.

It didn't really matter. Todd's frown had deepened into a scowl. "Vincent doesn't lie."

I gripped his shoulders, forcing him to look at me. "Don't you remember how you felt when Vincent first came? You hated him, you told me he was bad."

"I didn't mean it!" Todd struggled to escape. "Let me go, let me go! I'll tell Mommy to send you away, Cynda!"

I sat back on my heels and watched him scramble across the floor. Making him angry wasn't going to help. "I'm sorry, Toddy, I didn't mean to upset you."

He sat down a few feet away and picked up a little car. Without looking at me, he spun the front wheels listlessly.

"Would you like me to read to you?"

"I like the way Vincent reads better. I'll wait for him." Todd looked at the stairs longingly. "It's getting dark. Soon he'll come."

I left Todd sitting on the rug and went to the kitchen. Will's phone number was on the bulletin board beside the phone. I dialed quickly, praying he'd be home.

He answered on the second ring. "It's Cynda," I whispered. "Can you meet me at the shack?"

"When?"

"I'm leaving the inn now."

I was pulling on my parka when Todd appeared. "Where are you going, Cynda?"

"For a walk. Do you want to come with me?"

"I'm too tired."

I held out his jacket. "The fresh air will be good for you."

He hung back. "Wait for Vincent. All three of us can go. Wouldn't that be fun?"

"Vincent won't come downstairs till dinnertime, maybe not even then. You know how he is." While I talked, I stuffed Todd's arms into his sleeves. I zipped his jacket quickly, but when I tried to get him outside he resisted. It took all my strength to haul him across the threshold.

"The sun's too bright," he wailed. "It's hurting me, I can't see."

"Hush," I begged, tugging him across the snow. "Hush, Todd."

"Let me go," he sobbed. "I don't feel good."

We were beneath Vincent's window. I looked up fearfully, but the curtains were firmly closed. So far, we hadn't disturbed the creature's rest.

Ignoring Todd's protests, I picked him up and carried him away from the inn, stumbling through the snow, tripping, almost falling in my haste to escape unseen.

167

20

By the time we reached the shack, I was exhausted. Todd fought me every step of the way, hitting, slapping, and biting, howling, and swearing at me. I stumbled over the threshold and dropped him at Will's feet.

After Will bolted the door, he reached for Todd, but Todd pushed him away. "Don't touch me," he screamed. "I hate you!"

Will stared at my brother as if he couldn't believe his ears. "Todd," he said, "it's me, Will, your old buddy. Surely you don't believe I hurt Cynda, you don't think . . ."

Todd beat at the door. "I want to go home," he wailed. "Take me back, Cynda, take me back! I want Vincent!"

Between Todd's cries and the noise of the wind and the surf, I had to yell to be heard. "You've got to help me, Will. I've been such a fool, I've been so stupid. You tried to tell me, so did Todd. Now look at him, look at me. Why didn't I listen to you?"

Will was still staring at Todd, his face a study in horror and pity. Finally he turned to me. "What's wrong with him? What's wrong with you? What has Vincent done?"

"If I tell you, you won't believe me. You'll think I'm crazy, you'll say there's no such thing."

Will looked at me, his eyes steady, unblinking. The wind howled louder, the surf beat against the rocks below us. "The newspaper article you gave me," he said slowly. "The murderer—McThane—he looked just like Vincent, but how could that be? Eleanor Dunne was murdered more than sixty years ago."

"Vincent is, Vincent is . . ." I pressed my hands against my neck to dull the pain, but no matter how hard I tried I couldn't say the word. "Vincent seduced me," I sobbed at last. "He made me promise not to tell, but now he's seduced Todd, too. I have to tell, I can't let him take us away. He wants us to be his children, to live with him forever, become what he is, do what he does."

Afraid Will might not believe me, I pulled down the neck of my sweater and showed him the red mark, Vincent's love bite. "Todd has one just like this," I said.

Will drew in his breath. "Are you trying to tell me Vincent is a vampire?"

"Yes, yes," I cried, "that's what he is—a vampire! Vincent's a vampire!" I knew the word again, said it out loud, told the truth about Vincent. He was a vampire.

"That's why you bit me," Will said. "That's what you were trying to tell me."

169

Except for the wind and the surf, the shack was quiet. Todd slept by the door like a trapped animal, exhausted from his efforts to escape.

"What kills a vampire?" Will asked. "Sunlight? A stake through the heart?"

"Vincent says nothing can destroy him, he's too strong. Stakes and crosses, sunlight and garlic—he claims they're useless."

"There must be something we can do," Will muttered.

A gull swept past the window, crying into the wind, its wings white against the purple clouds. Soon the sun would set. Its light was gone from the east already. The sea was dark, the sky was dark. There was no line to mark where one ended and the other began.

Night would bring Vincent to me. He'd knock on my door, he'd enter my room, his face a mask of carved ivory, his eyes glittering with candlelight. Beautiful, he was beautiful, too beautiful to destroy. Too powerful. I couldn't fight him. It was futile to try.

Will touched my shoulder. "Think, Cynda, concentrate. Vincent must have a weak spot."

"Don't come close to me," I whispered, fearing the dark desire beating in my veins. "I can't trust myself not to . . ."

He looked at me as if he thought I might be joking, but he stepped back. Behind him, the fire crackled in the little stove.

"Fire," I whispered, remembering the day I'd

knocked the candle over. "I think Vincent's afraid of fire."

We gazed at each other, scarcely breathing. Will was the first to speak. "If I could force his car off the cliff . . . Maybe it would hit the rocks and explode, maybe he'd burn to a crisp."

"I could trick him into taking me for a ride," I said. "You could follow us in your truck. Then you could—"

"No," Will said sharply. "You'd go over the cliff with him, Cynda."

"I'd jump out before it went over the edge," I said quickly. "Like people do in movies."

How actors did things like that I had no idea, but it didn't matter. If I had to die to destroy Vincent, I would. Anything—even death—would be better than being his forever.

Will paced back and forth, thinking. Suddenly he stopped and pointed to the trapdoor. "Remember what I told you about the cave?"

I nodded, thinking of the dark and the damp and the smell of the sea far below.

"Bring Vincent here tonight," Will said in a low voice. "Use some excuse. I'll hide outside. While you're in the shack, I'll padlock the door so he can't open it."

He fumbled in his pocket and gave me a box of kitchen matches. My hands shook when I took them.

"Toss a lighted match into that pile of rags near

171

the stove. I'll soak them with turpentine. Hopefully Vincent won't notice; artists' studios always smell like oil paints and solvents."

"But how will I get out?"

"As soon as the fire starts, go to the trapdoor. I'll leave it open for you. Be sure and lock it behind you. There's a bolt. If we're lucky, Vincent will be trapped."

I clenched my fists against the pain. It was horrible to imagine Vincent's destruction, to picture him burning, writhing in pain and terror. He was so beautiful, so perfect, so clever. How could I kill him?

Will stared at me. "Is it too risky? Are you afraid? Maybe we shouldn't, maybe . . ."

"I don't know if I can do it," I sobbed. "He's strong, Will. It's hard to resist him."

By the door, Todd whimpered. He shivered, his hands and legs twitched. Leaping to his feet, he flung himself at the door. "It's dark, it's nighttime. We have to go home, Cynda. Vincent's waiting for us!"

I felt the same tug Todd felt, the same panic. We couldn't keep Vincent waiting. My hands shook as I zipped my jacket and pulled on my gloves. I was afraid, so afraid. Will's plan would never work. Todd and I were doomed.

"What's wrong, Cynda?"

"I'm scared."

"You can do it," Will said. "You have to."

Giving me a quick hug, he unlocked the door. Todd ran out into the cold, dark night, and I followed him.

Ahead was the inn. Its windows glowed with candles, summoning us to Vincent.

*

Susan met us at the kitchen door. "Where have you been?" She pulled Todd inside and glared at me. "You know he's sick, Cynda. How can you be so irresponsible?"

Once I would have defended myself, yelled back, accused her of blaming me for everything. Not tonight. Vincent stood in the hall behind her, head raised, eyes narrowed, watching me suspiciously.

"We went for a walk," I mumbled. "I forgot it gets dark so early."

"She took me to Will's shack," Todd whimpered. "He locked the door and kept us there. That's why we're late, he wouldn't let us go."

Susan's eyes widened. "You saw Will, Cynda? After what he did last night?"

Although I didn't look at Vincent, I felt his power. Against my will, I said, "We met him on the path, he took us to his shack, he tried, he tried—" I started crying. Vincent was forcing me to lie.

Susan murmured something, and Vincent stepped forward. "Perhaps you should call the police," he said. "The boy's obviously dangerous."

"Yes," Todd agreed. "Make the police put Will in jail, keep him there forever and ever. I'm scared of him. He tried to hurt Cynda."

"What's happened?" Dad joined us. He looked from Todd to me, then turned to Vincent.

173

Masking his cruel face with compassion, Vincent sighed. "It seems Will frightened Cynda and Todd this afternoon. I suggest you inform the police before something worse happens."

"No, it's not true," I whispered, "Don't believe him." My voice was inaudible to everyone but Vincent. His eyes met mine, dark and questioning. It was obvious he was furious with me.

When Dad picked up the phone, I ran to my room, planning to climb out the window and warn Will. Above me, the lamp went on in Vincent's room. In the oblong of light it cast on the snow, I saw his shadow. He was watching. If I went to Will, Vincent would follow me. He'd destroy us both.

I drew the curtains. Over my head, Vincent began to pace, back and forth, back and forth. He was waiting for night to fall, for the earth to darken and become his.

As restless as he, I flung myself into a chair. I tried to think, to plan, but, as usual, Vincent's footsteps came between me and my thoughts.

In despair, I went to Dad's study. I'd tell him the truth, I'd beg him to believe me, but just as I raised my hand to knock on his door, I heard a footstep on the stairs. Vincent stood on the landing, smiling down at me. Todd held his hand.

"You mustn't bother Daddy when he's writing," Todd said.

"That would be very foolish," Vincent agreed.

"Come here, Todd," I said, "I want to talk to you."

Vincent tightened his grip on my brother's hand. "I've promised to read to Todd till dinner's ready."

"*I'll* read to him." I ran up the stairs and grabbed Todd's other hand. "Come away from him, Toddy. Right now!"

Todd pulled his hand free. "Leave me alone, Cynda! You're not my real sister, I don't have to do anything you say. I hate you, I hate you!"

Todd's shrieks brought Susan to the foot of the steps. "What's going on?"

"Cynda yanked my arm, she hurt me," Todd cried. "Make her leave me alone, make her go back to her real mother. I don't want her to live here anymore."

I turned to Susan, trying to tell her, warn her, beg her to save us, but Vincent was too close. I felt his finger, sharp nailed and cold, trace my spine, his touch as light as frost on a window pane. Chilled into silence, I stared at Susan, imploring her to understand.

But she misread the message. "I know you don't feel well, Cynda. I know you're upset, but don't take it out on Todd. He's upset too, we all are. This business with Will is just heartbreaking. We never thought, never expected . . ."

Rubbing her forehead, Susan murmured, "Poor Mrs. Bigelow. I don't know how she'll bear it. She thinks the world of Will."

Vincent's fingernail pressed through my sweater like a shard of ice. His breath stirred the hair on the back of my neck. "It's a pity," he agreed softly. "Such a talented boy, nice-mannered, polite, handsome. Quite tragic really."

"I hate Will," Todd said. His voice was as cold and pitiless as Vincent's.

Susan stared at him. "Todd, what have I told you? It's wrong to hate people. Will is sick, he couldn't help what he did. He didn't mean to hurt Cynda, I'm sure he didn't. He couldn't have. Not Will."

"Now, now, Susan," Vincent said gently, "I know you were fond of the boy, but you mustn't allow your affection to cloud your judgment. Will might have done irreparable harm to Cynda. Be grateful we stopped him in time."

As he spoke, Vincent continued to run his finger up and down my spine. Numb, he was numbing me. I could barely focus my eyes. Nonetheless, I continued to stare at Susan, willing her to read my thoughts.

"Cynda," she said, "you and Todd look exhausted. Maybe you should both rest till dinner's ready."

Vincent moved his hand to my arm and squeezed it amiably, chilling me to the bone. "Perhaps you'd like to join Todd and me. We're going to read in front of the fire."

Todd opened his mouth to protest, but Vincent hushed him with a chuckle. "Shame on you, Toddy. You love your sister, you know you do. In fact, you love her so much you don't want to let her out of your sight."

As Vincent hoisted Todd to his shoulders, a look passed between them that made me shudder. Susan noticed nothing. Satisfied that we'd stopped quarreling, she'd already turned away.

"Come along, Cynda," Vincent said pleasantly.

Instead I hurried after Susan. "Don't you want me to help you with dinner, set the table, do something?"

"No, no." Susan gave me a quick hug. "Get some rest, Cynda."

Vincent smiled. From his perch on Vincent's shoulders, Todd smiled too. Like a prisoner, I followed them to the living room. Vincent settled himself on the couch and Todd climbed into his lap. Seizing my arm, he pulled me down beside him.

"Even if you told Susan the truth," he whispered, "she wouldn't believe you. Nevertheless, I have no intention of giving you the opportunity. Why take the risk?"

Todd eyed me coldly. "You're a tattletale, Cynda, but I'm not. I know how to keep secrets."

Vincent kissed Todd and Todd tilted his head back, exposing his throat. "Not now, Toddy," Vincent murmured. "Wait till later, when everyone's asleep."

"No," Todd begged. "Do it now, Vincent, I want you to."

I tried to pull Todd closer to me, but Vincent restrained me and hushed Todd at the same moment. "No more quarreling, children. We mustn't worry Susan."

Todd pouted for a few minutes but soon fell under the spell of Vincent's deep voice. "Once upon a time there was a kindly old wolf," the vampire began. "He lived alone in a beautiful mansion full of toys and candy, but he was very sad, he wanted some company, a dear little boy to love . . ."

Susan called us to dinner before Vincent reached the end of his tale. Patting Todd's head, he said, "We'll finish the story later, won't we?"

21

At the dinner table, I took a seat opposite Vincent. Whenever I raised my eyes, I met his dark stare. He seemed to be reassessing me, considering options, musing on my fate. There was a hungry look about him, an expectancy that made my neck ache. He meant to kill me, I was sure of it.

When the meal was over, we returned to the living room. Todd sat on Vincent's lap again, listening to him talk to Dad and Susan, showing no sign of boredom. He found Vincent as fascinating as I used to.

Save me, save him, I begged Dad. *Can't you see what Vincent is?*

But of course he couldn't. To Dad, Vincent was a fascinating, well-educated man, a sympathetic listener who understood the writing life. A charming fellow, a delightful guest.

Susan was no better. She sat by the fire sewing, her face rosy and innocent. Her earlier suspicions forgotten, she now doted on Vincent, offering him tea, sherry, claret, whatever he wished—her blood, I supposed, if he desired it.

Why can't you see? I shouted silently at them, my

head aching with wasted energy. *Why can't you wake up and help me?*

Vincent glanced at me and smiled. He heard my pleas, but he knew no else would.

A cold draft tickled the back of my neck. I turned to see if the window was open. It was shut tight. Outside, falling snow brightened the darkness. Driven by the wind, it hissed against the glass. A girl as pale as moonlight stood on the lawn, facing the inn. Shrouded in snow, she stretched her hands toward me. She wasn't alone. Behind her, barely visible, were the others. Like Eleanor Dunne, they reached out to me. Their white dresses swirled, their long hair streamed. The wind gave voice to their pain.

Without thinking, I flung the window open. "Eleanor," I cried, "Eleanor, help me!"

Dad and Susan leaped up, frightened by my behavior, but Vincent reached me first. He pushed me away from the window, pulled it shut, and fastened the latch, his eyes black with anger. As Dad rushed to help Vincent, I tried to break free of his hard, hurtful hands, but I was too weak. Vincent's sharp nails bit into my flesh, his pale, perfect skin glowed like the finest porcelain, his dark eyes told me there was no escape, no hope: *You can't defeat me. Neither can they. I'll do with you what I wish, little mouse.*

Exhausted, I slumped to the floor. It was useless to fight him. Not with Todd perched on the sofa, watching me pitilessly. Not with Dad and Susan leaning over me, blind to what was really happening. Only

Eleanor could help—but she and the others were shut outside in the dark, in the snow, in the merciless cold.

Soon I'd join them. I'd be one of the ghosts haunting Underhill, unseen and unheard till another girl came to the inn, unwittingly bringing Vincent with her.

Dad shook me, begging me to look at him. "Cynda, for God's sake, talk to me, tell me what's wrong!"

"Blame Will Bigelow for this," Vincent said angrily. "Your daughter's emotional health was so fragile, so delicate, Jeff. His attack has obviously traumatized Cynda."

"No," I sobbed, "not Will . . ."

Dad held me tighter, hushing me with reassurances. "Don't worry about Will Bigelow," he said bitterly. "He won't have a chance to hurt you ever again."

"No, Dad, you don't understand. Will, Will—" I couldn't go on. Vincent took my words before I could say them.

Susan knelt beside me. "Here, sip this." She pressed a glass against my lips. My mouth filled with brandy. I choked and sputtered; tears ran down my cheeks.

I let her help me to my feet, lead me to my room, undress me, tuck me into bed. "Sleep," Susan whispered. "Sleep, Cynda."

As soon as she left, I tiptoed to my window and quietly opened it. Snow blew into the room, whirling and spinning. The girls came with it. Silently, secretly, they circled me like snowflakes dancing on the wind.

Eleanor came close. Silently she touched the crimson spot on my neck. Her fingers burned my skin like dry ice. Slowly she pointed to her own neck and gestured at the other girls. They surrounded me. Each bore Vincent's mark, the only color on their skin, drops of blood on fallen snow.

The wind blew through the open window. Crying for vengeance, it filled my room with phantoms. "No peace," it moaned. "No rest for us, no rest for you."

Behind me, Vincent strode into the room, carrying Todd on his shoulders. The girls vanished into the darkness outside, blown away like wraiths of smoke. Eleanor was the last to go.

Vincent shut the window. "What did I tell you?" he hissed. "They're ghosts, phantoms. They have no strength, they can do nothing. I took all their blood, I gave them none of mine."

Tipping his head, he smiled at Todd. "What shall we do with your half sister, Toddy? Do we still want her in our family? Or shall we send her to join her friends out there in the dark?"

Todd considered the question. How pale he was, how thin. Vincent had taken more than his blood; he'd robbed him of happiness, of innocence. My brother was an empty husk. I ached for him, but there was no mercy in his blue eyes.

"Throw her in the ocean," he said in his new

voice, cold and spooky, almost as inhuman as Vincent's. "That's what you did to the others."

Vincent grinned. "What a marvelous boy you are. I shall never grow tired of you, Toddy."

Like a good father, Vincent fetched our coats and gloves, scarves and hats. "Bundle up, children," he said gently, but his eyes mocked me. "You wouldn't want to catch your death in the cold."

The three of us went out into the stormy night, Todd riding Vincent's shoulders, me stumbling beside him, his strong hand clasping mine. In seconds, the inn vanished, candles and all, behind a wall of falling snow.

Every now and then the veils of snow parted, giving me glimpses of Eleanor and the others. They filled the air around us. Ahead, behind, on all sides, they seemed to guide us through the night.

The wind carried their voices to me. *Vengeance*, it cried, *vengeance*.

If Vincent saw or heard them, he gave no sign. Despite the knee-deep snow, he walked tirelessly, dragging me after him. I was weak, exhausted. If I fell I wouldn't get up, I'd lie still and let the snow bury me. But Eleanor wouldn't allow that. Although Vincent seemed unaware of her, I felt her near me, helping me, urging me to be brave and strong.

We started down the path to the ocean. Beneath the roar of the wind, I heard the surf pound the rocks. Just ahead was Will's shack. Candles flickered in the windows. Wood smoke curled from the chimney, mingling its smell with the sea air. It looked warm and cozy. Perhaps Will was there after all, waiting for us.

"What is that building?" Vincent studied the shack, curious as always.

"It's Will's studio," Todd said. "He must be in there. He'll see us, Vincent, he'll know."

Vincent hushed Todd. "Suppose we sneak up on Will and surprise him? If we're very clever, Toddy, we can make it look like Will killed Cynda, then himself."

"No, Todd," I cried, horrified to see my brother smile. "Will's our friend, he's always been good to you, surely you wouldn't want to harm him."

Todd scowled at me. "That was a long time ago," he said, hugging Vincent. "I've only got one friend now—Vincent."

"That's right," Vincent said. "And don't forget it, son. I'd hate for you to disappoint me the way Cynda has."

Vincent placed his finger against Todd's lips to silence his protests. Taking care to make no noise, he stalked through the snow. Todd leaned forward, his face eager. Unwillingly I followed, my hand crushed in Vincent's. I prayed Will had done the things he'd promised.

With Todd clinging to his neck, Vincent kicked the door open. The shack was empty, but the stove glowed with heat. The candle flames streamed in the wind, but they did not go out.

"Your father's call to the police must have resulted

184

in Will's arrest," Vincent said smugly. Putting Todd down, he walked around the shack, examining the few paintings Will had left on the walls. Rough sketches, most of them. Not his best work, but still impressive.

"The boy has real talent," Vincent murmured approvingly. "Perhaps you'd rather have a brother than a sister, Toddy."

Todd frowned. "I don't want a brother or a sister," he said. "I want to be your only child so you'll always love me best."

Vincent turned to me, smiling, beautiful, perfect in his evil. "Poor Cynda, such a hateful half brother. You need comforting, don't you?"

Without warning, he seized me and forced my head back. His teeth found the mark on my throat. As he bit into my flesh, Todd cried out angrily and hurled himself between us.

"Don't kiss Cynda—kiss me, Vincent!" he yelled.

Taken by surprise, Vincent laughed and released me. "Don't be so impatient, Toddy. I have a big appetite."

Now, the wind cried, *now*.

Stumble-legged with fear, I grabbed Todd and ran toward the trapdoor hidden in the shadows behind the stove.

"Let me go!" Todd screamed. "What are you doing? Vincent, help me!"

Apparently amused, Vincent said, "Bite her, Toddy. Show her how sharp your teeth are."

He clearly didn't consider me a threat. No need to

be alarmed, no need to stop me. Where could I go? What could I do? As far as Vincent knew, I was trapped.

It was his overconfidence that made it possible for me to pull the matches out of my pocket. Before he or Todd realized what I was doing, I struck a handful and hurled them into the rags Will had left near the stove. At the same moment, a gust of wind toppled the candles, and a wall of fire leaped up between Vincent and me.

Shocked by the flames, Todd forgot about biting me and redoubled his efforts to escape. "Vincent," he screamed. "Vincent!"

Shielding his face from the fire, Vincent leaped back. "Stop, Cynda," he shouted. "I command you!"

My neck throbbed. I felt weak, dizzy. I couldn't let Vincent die. Not like this.

As I hesitated, the wind rose. They were out there in the dark and the cold, Eleanor and the others, lost until every drop of their blood was burned from Vincent's veins. They whirled around the shack, begging me to destroy him, to save them, to give them peace.

Holding Todd tight, I groped for the trapdoor. If Will hadn't left it open, I wouldn't have had the strength to lift it. Weak with terror, I yanked my brother down the ladder with me.

"Todd," Vincent cried, "make her stop. I love you, you love me. You're mine, mine! Don't let Cynda destroy us!"

Todd writhed and twisted, cursing me and crying

for Vincent. Praying we wouldn't fall, I pulled the trapdoor shut and slid the bolt home.

Over our heads, the fire roared. I felt the heat through the door. From the inferno, Vincent screamed—a horrible sound, worse than anything I'd ever heard or imagined. It raced through my veins, scalding my blood as if it were being consumed by invisible flames.

"Cynda," Todd sobbed, "Cynda, what have you done?" His voice rose to a high, keening wail almost as chilling as Vincent's. "The fire's inside me, it's killing me, too!"

The air was too hot to breathe. Smoke blinded me, choked me. Clinging to the ladder, I peered into the damp, sea-breathing darkness below. "We have to climb down, Todd."

He gripped a rung and shook his head. "No," he sobbed. "No. I hate you! You killed him, now you want to kill me!"

I felt him tremble. He was too weak to fight me, too exhausted to move. Cautiously I edged past him and began to feel my way down with my feet, begging Todd to follow me. The ladder swayed under our weight. Its rungs were wet and slippery, but the air rushing up to meet us was cold and damp and sweet.

At the bottom, I held Todd tight and let him cry. "We're safe," I whispered again and again. "We're safe, Toddy. He can't come after us, he can't hurt us."

Finally Todd stopped crying and looked at me. His eyes were alive again, the cold hatred gone, washed away by tears. "Is Vincent dead? Did he burn up in the fire?"

"Yes," I said. "Yes, he's dead."

Todd shuddered as if he'd just awakened from a bad dream. "Vincent bit me," he said, touching his neck. "He made me do bad things, he made me say bad things. He made me think bad thoughts about you and Mommy and Daddy." Tears filled his eyes again. "How can anyone love me now, Cynda?"

I smoothed his hair and kissed him. "It wasn't your fault, Toddy. Nobody will blame you. Vincent was bad, evil. He was a—"

"Vampire." Todd blurted out the word. "Vincent was a *vampire*. He bit us, he took our blood, he wanted to kill you. And so did I, I wanted what he wanted . . ." He broke into loud sobs and buried his face in my neck. "I'm sorry, Cynda, I'm sorry. I don't want you to be dead, you're my sister, I love you."

"I know, Toddy, I know. I love you too." I rocked him in my arms to comfort him. "Vincent was so strong, so clever. He knew just what to tell us. I believed his lies just like you did."

Still weeping, Todd nestled closer. Glad for his warmth, I held him tight. Gradually he relaxed. His body went limp, his breathing deepened.

While my brother slept, I stared into the darkness. Vincent was dead, I told myself. His spell was broken, his power destroyed. Todd was himself again. So was I. When we were strong enough, we'd leave the cave, go back to the inn, and live our lives as if we'd never known Vincent. At least we'd try. . . .

22

I'm not sure how long Todd slept. When he woke up, I tried to lead him to the cave's entrance, but it was dark and the rocks were slippery. I hadn't thought to bring a flashlight, and the matches Will had given me flickered and went out as soon as I lit them. The surf boomed, reminding me how easily we could drown.

Suddenly Todd grabbed my arm. "Look, Cynda, a light. Someone's coming."

My first thought was Vincent—he'd returned like a creature in a horror movie, springing upon us just when we thought we were safe. Todd must have feared the same thing for he flung his arms around me and began to sob.

The light came closer, closer. Its beam lit the rocks and shone in our eyes, blinding us. Will ran toward us, calling our names. For a few seconds we couldn't speak. We all clung to one another, laughing and crying.

"I was so scared," Will said at last. "The police kept me for hours. I thought I was too late, I was afraid you and Todd . . ."

I gasped. "The door—you weren't here to lock it, Will. What if Vincent escaped?"

We stared at each other. Had we failed after all? I'd been so sure Vincent was dead. I'd felt him burn, shared his agony, known when it ended. So had Todd.

"Let's get out of here." Will handed me the flashlight and lifted Todd to his shoulders. The three of us made our way slowly and cautiously over the rocks. The sea slapped at us, waves rumbled and surged, driven into the cave by the wind. Todd whimpered in fear, but we found our way safely to the trail and climbed to the top of the cliffs.

Nothing was left of the shack but ashes and charred wood licked by tiny flames. Silently we watched the fire dancing in the wind, flaring up here, dying there, glowing like Christmas lights in the falling snow. Despite the crackle and pop of the fire, despite the wind and the surf, the night seemed incredibly still.

Suddenly Will put Todd down and ran to the shack. For a moment, his body was a black shape against the firelight. He bent, picked something up from the snow, and brought it to me.

"It's the padlock," he whispered, "and the hasp. Someone locked the door, Cynda. Someone made sure Vincent couldn't escape."

While Will examined the lock, I stared into the darkness, listening for voices in the wind. Snowflakes as shy and cold as airborne kisses touched my cheek. I glimpsed pale faces, blowing veils of hair, hands lifted in farewell. Then Eleanor and the others were gone, drifting away like fog. The wind dropped. The night was still and peaceful.

"Goodbye," I whispered. "Goodbye."

Will looked at me, puzzled. "Who are you talking to?"

"Didn't you see them?"

He shook his head and picked up Todd again. He'd seen no one. Neither had Todd. Turning our backs on the fire, we trudged toward the inn.

"What will we tell your father?" Will asked. "How will we explain Vincent's death?"

"Say he was a bad man," Todd said fiercely. "Say he told lies, say he hurt Cynda and me, say we burned him up in a fire. Say he deserved it."

I squeezed my brother's hand. He yawned and rested his cheek on Will's cap. By the time we reached the inn, Todd was asleep. He looked like himself again, rosy and healthy, an ordinary little boy.

Before I went inside, I looked up at Vincent's window. His room was dark, the curtains hung motionless, but it was hard to believe he wasn't standing behind them, watching us come home. I expected him to fling the curtains aside and say, "Surely you didn't think you'd get rid of me so easily."

With the memory of his laughter ringing in my ears, I ran past the mound of snow burying the Porsche and raced up the steps ahead of Will and Todd. When I opened the kitchen door, I heard Dad shouting into the phone. "I tell you they're missing,

191

both of them. I don't care how bad the roads are, get out here and help me find them! By morning it may be too late. For God's sake, it may already be too late!"

"Daddy, Daddy," Todd cried. Will set him on the floor and he ran into the inn with us close behind.

Dad's face lit up with joy. He dropped the phone and gathered us close. Susan leaped up from the table and threw herself into the hugs and kisses. It was a long time before anyone remembered the phone, still swinging on the end of its cord, beeping with alarm.

"Where have you been?" Susan cried.

"Where's Vincent?" Dad asked at the same moment.

I clung to Dad and wept. "He took us to Will's shack, he tried to hurt us. There was a fire, Daddy. It was horrible, terrible . . ."

"Vincent was a bad, bad man," Todd sobbed. "I told you and told you. Why didn't you listen, Daddy?"

Dad held Todd tighter and turned to Will, his face agonized. "My God," he whispered, "I believed Vince, I thought you—how could I have been such a fool?"

"Oh, Will," Susan wept, "we're so sorry. I don't know what was wrong with us. It's as if, as if . . ."

Will let Susan hug him. He looked close to tears himself.

By the time the police arrived, Susan had made a pot of peppermint tea and we were gathered around the kitchen table, afraid to let one another out of our sight. We'd stopped crying, but we were far from calm.

Sergeant Jackson had many questions, but her voice was soft and pleasant and she seemed genuinely sympathetic. She listened to the same story we'd told Dad and Susan. Her assistant wrote down every word carefully, stopping every now and then to verify things. He seemed puzzled by how little any of us knew about Vincent.

When she'd gotten all the information she wanted from us, we took her upstairs to Vincent's room, while the assistant phoned the station to check out the car's license plate number. All Sergeant Jackson found were two neatly folded black sweaters, spare socks and underwear, a tweed jacket, two shirts, and a pair of slacks. On Vincent's writing table were stacks of second-hand books and sheets of paper covered with illegible scribbling. If he'd had money or credit cards, a driver's license or a Social Security card, he'd carried them in the pockets of the clothes he wore to the shack.

The policewoman led the way downstairs. Even though I knew Vincent was gone, I feared the darkness at my back. Suppose I looked over my shoulder and saw his pale face watching us from the shadows?

To no one's surprise, the Porsche had been stolen several weeks ago in New York. "That explains why Mr. Morthanos never left the inn," Sergeant Jackson said.

At the bottom of the steps, I moved closer to Dad. He was trying to answer one last question from

Sergeant Jackson. She still didn't understand how Vincent had managed to kidnap Todd and me.

"It's hard to explain," Dad admitted. "It seems Susan and I dozed off. We couldn't have been asleep for more than a few minutes but when we opened our eyes the living room was empty. Todd and Vincent were gone."

Dad's voice broke and Susan went on for him. "We'd put Cynda to bed earlier, she'd been upset. When we went to her room, our children were gone and the window was wide open."

"We saw tracks in the snow," Dad added, "signs of a struggle."

"It was as if a spell had lifted," Susan said. "We looked at each other and we knew, we *knew* Vincent had taken our son and daughter."

"Our children . . . our son and daughter." Susan's and Dad's words rang in my ears. Not our stepdaughter, but *our daughter, our children*. I leaned against Dad's shoulder and he put his arm around me reassuringly.

Although she still seemed puzzled, Sergeant Jackson thanked us for our cooperation. Before she and her assistant left, she said, "We have two officers at the fire. Perhaps they'll discover something useful when the ashes cool."

Todd edged closer and took my hand. I felt him tremble. "You won't find anything," he whispered.

It was the first time he'd spoken since the police arrived, so he had everyone's attention. "Vincent's just ashes now, nothing's left of him," he said. "That's what happens when vampires die."

Will and I looked at each other uneasily, but Dad pulled Todd onto his knee. "Vincent was a wicked man, Todd. He hurt you and Cynda, but he wasn't a vampire, son. Vampires are imaginary. They aren't real."

Sergeant Jackson nodded. "In a case like this," she said softly, "counseling is a good idea. I'd be happy to recommend someone."

Susan began to cry again and Dad held Todd tighter. Sergeant Jackson wrote down a name and left it by the phone. She and her assistant said their goodbyes and left. Will followed them into the snowy night, pausing in the doorway to promise he'd see us soon.

After Susan took Todd to bed, Dad clasped my hands. "I don't know why I didn't see, didn't guess. You and Todd are so precious to me, I love you so much, yet I let Vincent—"

He released my hand and struck the table with his fist. "How could I have trusted that man?"

I was tempted to tell my father the truth, but perhaps it was better to let him go on believing Vincent was depraved, a pervert of some kind, a child abuser. If Dad believed he'd invited a creature from myth and legend to cross his threshold, he'd have to rethink his entire concept of reality. I wasn't sure he was ready for that.

Putting my arms around him, I whispered, "I

believed Vincent too, Daddy. He was very clever. He knew just what we wanted to hear."

*

One afternoon several weeks later, I sat on the couch, reading a letter from Mom. Dad had told her about Vincent and she wanted to be sure I was all right. "Please come to Italy," she begged. "Steve and I would love to have you—even if it's just for a visit."

I refolded the letter and slid it back into the envelope. I missed Mom, but I was just beginning to feel comfortable with Dad. If I left now, I might not have another chance to get to know him. Soon I'd be in college. After that I'd be on my own. Things wouldn't be the same then.

Maybe next winter when it was cold and gray in Maine I'd go to Italy, but for now I wanted to stay here. With Vincent gone, Underhill was quiet and peaceful. A fire crackled on the hearth. Ebony dozed beside me, purring contentedly. Susan's sewing machine whirred. Dad's printer *rat-tat-tatted* in his den. Mrs. Bigelow's vacuum cleaner rumbled back and forth across the floor overhead.

At my feet, Todd played with his castle, calling out knightly challenges in a fierce voice. Catching my eye, he scrambled onto the sofa. "Will you read me a story, Cynda?"

I took a book from a pile of old favorites, and Todd leaned against me, sighing contentedly. After a few minutes, he startled me by reaching up to touch the small scar on my neck. For a second, it tingled the way it used to. Against my will, I remembered dark, mocking eyes, strong hands, sharp teeth sinking into my throat.

"Are you sure it's over?" Todd whispered. "Are you absolutely positive Vincent won't come back?"

Something in my brother's voice worried me. I stared into his eyes, as blue as ever but not quite as innocent. Deep in their depths, a shadow lurked, a memory. A memory I shared.

"He promised we'd live forever," Todd said dreamily. "We'd do what we pleased. No rules. He'd always love us best."

"We'd never be lonely. We'd never be sad," I added softly. "We'd be his children, he'd never leave us."

We stared at each other, scared to realize we were still tempted by the things Vincent had promised. Across the room, his empty chair faced us silently. I told myself he'd never sit there again. Someday we'd forget which chair had been his, we'd forget which room had been his. I'd stop expecting to hear his footsteps overhead. I'd forget his eyes, his kisses, his promises. He was gone forever. I had to believe that.

"Everything Vincent promised was a lie," I reminded Todd, my brother, myself. "He was bad, evil."

Todd nodded, his face solemn. "He wanted us to be like him. But we aren't."

Fighting my own uncertainty, I said fiercely, "That's right, Toddy. We aren't like Vincent and we never will be."

He seemed satisfied. Picking another book, he said, "Read this one now. Make sure the wolf falls down the chimney and lands in the boiling water. Make sure the pig eats him up. Every single bit. I don't want anything left—not even one hair."

I opened the book and began. "Once upon a time there were three little pigs."

Just as I read, "Little Pig, Little Pig, let me come in," I heard a knock on the back door. A shiver raced across my skin, and Todd clutched my arm, his eyes wide. We both held our breath till Susan welcomed Will inside.

Todd looked at me and laughed. "Keep reading, Cynda. Will likes this story, too."

I guess my brother was right because Will sat down beside me and snuggled as close as Todd to hear what happened next.